PRAISE FOR SAM CHEEVER

Sam Cheever creates some of the best characters you could ever find in the pages of a book.

— SENSUALREADS.COM

Ms. Cheever writes with class, humor and lots of fun while weaving an excellent story.

— THE ROMANCE STUDIO

Sticks and stones can break my bones, but wrinkles might actually kill me!

Just when I think I understand life, the Universe flings a magic booger at me.

It just doesn't pay to think you've got a handle on things. For example, my favorite customer, Mrs. Foxladle, got into a simple disagreement with her book club friends over their obsession with youth and beauty. The next thing you know, they're all dead. Did Mrs. Foxladle kill them?

It certainly seems like a possibility. But I'm still holding on to the hope that I'm dealing with a rogue magical artifact in the hands of someone with diabolical intent. Unfortunately, I haven't been able to figure out what it is and who's wielding it with deadly results.

I was counting on Detective Grym, a real rock of a guy, to help me find the culprits. But Grym's life-span just turned unpredictable. (You could say things are a bit rocky for him right now.) Which leaves solving the mystery up to me and my friends.

It's just a really good thing I have a cat and a frog and... Yeah, about that... I'm really no closer to figuring out how to use *them* either.

Holy goblin phlegm!

This magic wrangling stuff is hard!

GRAM CROAKIES

SAM CHEEVER

ELECTRIC PROSE PUBLICATIONS

YOUTH BEFORE BEAUTY!

*T*ucking an errant strand of long brown hair behind one ear, I took a sip of my quickly cooling tea and focused on my notes from the last artifact I'd wrangled. I'd been trying lately to do a better job of journaling my adventures in the hopes that it would help me get better at my job.

I had a *lot* of room to improve in that area.

The bell on the door to Croakies jangled. My cat, Mr. Wicked trotted from the back of the bookstore and jumped up onto the counter in front of me, his orange gaze fixed on the man who'd just entered the store.

Detective Wise Grym stood just inside the door, a large metal box clutched in his hands and rain dripping from his dark hair.

"Ribbit!" Mr. Slimy said from his place inside the glass fish tank I'd placed on a table near the counter.

He hopped over a shiny collection of smooth rocks and flung himself against the glass as if he wanted to welcome the detective himself.

Or give him warts.

Given the fact that the frog was still serving as a squishy green bus for one arrogant witch with trust issues where law enforcement was concerned, it could easily be the latter.

As if reading my thoughts, a misty, semi-transparent haze rose from the frog and settled onto the carpet, depositing a ghost witch alongside the fish tank. "What's gargoyle man doing here?" Rustin asked snottily.

I fought a roll of my eyes at the demeaning reference to Grym's magical form. Grym had asked me not to tell anybody what he was, but since only a very small group of people could see or hear the ghost witch, I'd felt like it was okay to tell him.

My assistant Sebille, the city Sprite, had experienced Grym's form first hand. She'd been there on that rooftop with me when the gargoyle had taken on the dragon, whose miniaturized form had once filled the box he was holding in his hands.

I took a beat to enjoy the view.

The Detective was just under six feet tall with broad shoulders, dark-caramel eyes, and mahogany brown hair with golden streaks where the sun had bleached it. His square jaw and sharply cut cheekbones could have been carved from stone.

In fact, sometimes they were.

"Detective Grym. You finally brought my box back." A week late.

Wise Grym took one look at my red-rimmed blue eyes and frowned. "Are you sick?"

I barely kept from grimacing. I was sick all right. Sick of trying to co-exist with a noisy, messy, bossy Sprite whose promised "temporary" habitation in my beloved private space was going on ten days, three hours, forty-one minutes, and twenty-three seconds.

Make that twenty-four seconds.

Twenty-five...

I couldn't sleep because of Sebille's whistling snores, and I hadn't gotten to watch my favorite television shows more than a handful of times since she'd moved in with me. I'm not even going to mention the ridiculous, claustrophobic chaos of having all her furniture stuffed into my small place alongside mine. Okay, I mentioned it, but it's not my fault. The mess was making me cray!

The worst part of it all was that Sebille didn't seem to care a whit about looking for a new place to live. She seemed perfectly happy cooking her foul-smelling concoctions on my stove and snoring on her couch in my living room. The only peace I ever seemed to get anymore was when the bossy Sprite went next door to visit with her mother, the Queen of the Fae, who was living in my friend

Lea's greenhouse in the lot behind of our two shops.

I dropped my pen and came around the short counter, moving toward the handsome detective with a finger against my lips.

His frown deepened.

"Hello, Detective. How are you?"

He shook his head, not understanding my warning to silence.

"You've outdone yourself this time, hon," Mrs. Foxladle said, coming around the end of the shelving for the mystery aisle with four paperbacks piled in her arms. "I want to thank you for pointing me toward the *Bewildered Basset Mysteries*. I find I quite enjoy them, despite the fact that the cat has second-place billing to the hound..." She jerked to a stop when she laid eyes on the Detective, a sly grin curving her lips. "Well, hello there, young man."

Grym shuffled from foot to foot under the older woman's assessing gaze. But I think it was probably the wink she threw me, as if Grym and I were an item, that discombobulated him the most.

"Mrs. Foxladle, this is Detective Grym," I told her. "He's the one who told me about the Basset Mysteries." I threw him a bright smile. "Aren't you, Detective?"

Of course, that was a lie...a dang lie...and his quick glare was almost more fun than my anticipation of his response.

"Um. Yes. I...erm...love those books," Grym stuttered out.

Mrs. Foxladle leaned a fleshy hip against the shelves, a gleam in her eyes. "How fun! Which one do you like best, Detective? I'll read that one next."

My smile widened as I anticipated the verbal calisthenics Grym would need to employ to get out of answering her question.

But he surprised me by looking as if he were actually considering the query. "That's a really hard question for me," he told Mrs. Foxladle.

I almost laughed. I just bet it was.

"Book one was predictably the weakest story, plot-wise, but I have to say I loved the characters so much in that one. I particularly thought Basil was charming. And Penelope was irresistible. Book two, *Befuddled Basil Baulks*, had a much better story but I thought the author lost a bit of her love of Basil and Pene's relationship in the mix."

I felt my mouth falling open but was helpless to stop it, despite the smug glance the detective sent my way.

Before he'd even completed his astounding assertion, Mrs. Foxladle's gaze had lost its teasing glint, and she was nodding with excitement. "My thoughts exactly," she told him, tugging a book out of the pile. "Have you read the third one yet?"

Grym nodded, pointing to the book. "I think you'll be pleasantly surprised. The author managed to meld the best aspects of the first two books and came up with a really strong mystery premise in three."

Mrs. Foxladle jittered happily, her eyes sparkling with pleasure. "It's so much fun to meet another mystery connoisseur," she told him happily. "I wonder," The elderly book lover reached into her purse and pulled out a small, white rectangle, handing it to Grym. "Would you like to join our book club, Detective? It would be ever so much fun discussing the mysteries with a real, live police detective."

He paled, his gaze spinning to mine, filled with panic. "Um..."

I decided I'd teased him enough. "Why don't we get you checked out, Mrs. Foxladle," I told my favorite customer. "I'm sure Detective Grym needs to get back to work."

"Of course." She patted his hand. "I'm so sorry to have kept you." But before she followed me across to the register, she tucked the card into the pocket of his jacket, winking coyly. "I hope you'll join us, Detective."

He gave her a smile, nodding. "Thanks for the invitation. It's very kind."

Grym disappeared between the bookshelves as I was checking out Mrs. Foxladle and I thought he was probably hiding among the reference books hoping to avoid more pressure from the kindly old woman. But her comment about book club reminded me. "It's Tuesday. Aren't you supposed to be at book club tonight?" I asked as I handed over her purchases.

Wicked rubbed against her arm as she took her bag, purring loudly when she scratched between his dark gray ears.

Mrs. Foxladle's lip curled slightly at my question. "I decided to skip this week, hon. I didn't care for the book we were discussing at all."

"Oh, that's too bad. I know how much you enjoy those meetings."

She shrugged, her expression darkening for just a moment before she forced a smile onto her face. "I wish everyone was as considerate of people's feelings as you are, Naida." She patted my hand and turned away, her steps not quite as lively as usual.

I watched her go, feeling as if there was something wrong in her world and wishing I could fix it. "Goodnight, Mrs. Foxladle."

"Goodnight, hon." She lifted her head, gaze focused on the shelves of books running the depth of the store. "Goodbye, Detective."

She didn't wait for him to respond, which was a good thing because Grym didn't emerge from the stacks for a couple of minutes. And when he did, his expression wasn't happy.

I noticed that the card she'd given him was

clutched in his hand. "What's wrong?" I asked, coming out from behind the counter.

His gaze slid to me, worry darkening the melted caramel color to dull brown.

I pointed to the card. "Are you considering joining the book club?" I grinned to show him I was teasing, but he didn't grin back.

Ice formed on my spine. "What's wrong, Grym?"

He handed me the metal box and lifted Mrs. Foxladle's card, showing it to me. "This address..."

I tried to see the address on the card, but his fingers obscured the text on the front. "What about it?"

The detective looked at the white rectangle again, shifting his fingers so he could read the information typed on its surface. He shook his head, swallowing before answering. "It's why I came here tonight. There's been a magical incident." He lifted his focus from the card, his gaze haunted. "Five ladies. The landlady told me they had book club every Tuesday evening."

The ice spread until my lungs were frozen and I had trouble taking a deep breath. My hand was suddenly covering my mouth. "An artifact?"

"It has to be," he told me. "Nothing else could have done what..." He swallowed hard again as his gaze slid to the door. "Her friends are all..."

I made a soft sound, turning my gaze toward the door again. "Poor Mrs. Foxladle," I murmured.

Grym nodded, finally seeming to shake off his horror, his gaze tightening as it settled on me. "Will you come to the scene? I'd really like your opinion. And if the artifact is still in the apartment..."

I nodded. "Of course. Let me just tell Sebille I'm stepping out."

There were no bodies in the room.

In fact, to my eye, there wasn't really much at all to point to murder or even natural death. I stood back as Grym closely examined the floor around the table and then bent with a magnifying glass to scrutinize the seat of each chair in turn.

Watching from a couple of feet away, I squinted at the spot where he was looking and saw nothing. Except maybe a tiny spot in the center of the chair, which just looked like a food crumb to me.

I cast my gaze around the place, noting the abundance of upholstered furniture covered in chintz fabric and glossy wood tables protected by what looked like homemade doilies.

The room smelled like a combination of lemon dusting spray and the sweet scent of lilacs from an overflowing vase filled with fresh flowers at a nearby table.

The table Grym was perusing appeared to be an

inexpensive rectangular folding table, covered in a flowery tablecloth that hung nearly to the floor on the long sides. Six metal folding chairs were arranged around it, only one of them still pushed up under the table.

I blinked rapidly as I realized that had to be Mrs. Foxladle's place. It was a miracle she'd decided not to attend the meeting that night. As far as I knew, she rarely missed book club.

I checked out the surface of the table, seeing a teacup filled with varying levels of cooling tea at each place. The cups were painted with pastel flowers, and each one had a tiny bee painted into the inside, looking as if it was climbing toward the lip. They were adorable.

"It doesn't look like they had time to drink their tea," I offered helpfully.

Each place setting also sported a well-worn paperback. I smiled sadly when I recognized the bookmarks I'd had done with depictions of Mr. Wicked and Mr. Slimy inside a couple of them.

A plate that looked as if it had been loaded up with baked goods was empty except for one small muffin and some crumbs. I wondered if the muffins had been poisoned.

Each setting had a small plate nearby, more crumbs attesting to the fact that the ladies had enjoyed a nice snack before they...

I swallowed hard.

Next to one plate was a grease spot that probably came from an unwrapped muffin or maybe a cookie. That particular plate had no crumbs, as if the person sitting there had either foregone the snack or had dropped the muffin onto the tablecloth instead, creating the grease spot.

If the ladies who'd been in that room really did turn up dead or missing, I didn't envy Grym's job trying to figure out what had happened. "Are you sure the women didn't just leave?" I asked Grym. "Who reported them missing?"

Grym straightened, his expression tight. "They didn't leave." He scanned a glance around the room.

"But then where are their bodies?"

Instead of answering me, he frowned more deeply.

"Detective?"

He shook his head and moved to the table, using the magnifying glass on the items scattered across the top while ignoring my questions.

"I can't help if you won't talk to me."

He continued to ignore me, his focus locked on his search.

I sighed. Stepping back from the table, I tugged my keeper magic forward and lifted my hands, sending the energy into the air and watching as several thin gray ribbons of magic wove away from my fingers and slithered throughout the apartment, disappearing from sight.

There were no chimes of discovery.

One strand headed for the table and wound around the remaining muffin before sliding across the table, hesitating on the grease spot, and then wrapping around Grym's arm like a bracelet.

He lifted a scowl in my direction.

"Oops! Sorry," I said, giving him an embarrassed smile. "Just trying to help."

He straightened, shaking his arm to dispel the ribbon of magic. It dissipated with a soft hiss as he headed in my direction. "Don't touch anything."

I frowned. "I haven't touched anything..."

He handed me the magnifying glass. "The seats of the chairs."

Grym stared at me for a moment as I realized he was answering my questions. "Ah. Show, don't tell," I said, nodding. "Got it."

I moved to the closest chair and leaned over it, focusing the magnifying glass over the seat as he'd done, and saw... "There's nothing here."

He frowned, taking the glass from my hand and giving the seat a long examination. "Hm," he said. His glance skimmed to the paperback, teacup, and empty plate at that spot.

The detective moved to the next chair, looking up after just a moment. "This one."

I took the glass again and bent over the seat, focusing it on the tiny speck I saw at the very center of the vinyl.

The "spot" was actually comprised of two things, a tiny, lima-bean-shaped clump of something lying in a pool of liquid. I moved the magnifying glass closer and squinted at the teeny, tiny...

I jumped back with a yelp, dropping the glass as I stumbled backward, putting as much distance as I could between me and the object on that chair. My horrified gaze lifted to Grym's finding its match on his face. "Holy alligator pajamas."

He nodded. "Do you see why I believe it's a magical artifact?"

I nodded, my gaze sliding back to the chair as dizziness swamped me. My heart was pounding so hard in my chest, I thought I might pass out. "Please tell me that wasn't what I thought it was."

"I wish I could, Naida Keeper." He scrubbed a big hand over his bristly jaw, sending the scratchy sound of whiskers against skin into the painfully silent room. "But I'm pretty sure that whatever killed those women, did it by returning them to their earliest possible forms."

"The ultimate anti-aging product," I murmured in revulsion, as my heart tried to bang its way through my ribs.

2

FROM THE BEGINNING...

I stood behind Grym and looked around at the row of well-maintained buildings along the street. The neighborhood of tall, slender stone and brick buildings had undergone gentrification a few years earlier, returning a once-proud area back to its former, elegant glory.

Mrs. Foxladle had lived in her home since well before the restoration. I remembered her complaining about the noise and mess of the work in the early days of the improvements.

Despite her unhappiness at having her world turned topsy-turvy around her, even Mrs. Foxladle couldn't argue with the results.

At that time of night, the streets were quiet, the residents tucked into their homes behind closed drapes, backlit by the soft yellow glow of interior lights.

Grym rang the bell and a musical chime sang out inside the home. We waited as soft footfalls sounded behind the glossy, pale green door.

"Who is it?" Mrs. Foxladle's warbly voice asked.

"Detective Grym of the Enchanted police, ma'am."

"Oh. Just a moment, please."

Grym glanced at me as the sound of locks disengaging announced Mrs. Foxladle's compliance.

I grimaced. I really wasn't looking forward to telling the elderly woman that her friends had been found dead.

She tugged the door open a crack and peered out at Grym. "Hello again. I'm sorry, but can I see your credentials, please?"

He tugged the badge from inside his sweater and held it up for her to see.

"What is this about, Detective?" Mrs. Foxladle asked, worry threading her voice.

"May we come inside, ma'am?" he asked.

"We?"

I took a deep breath at her uncertain query and peeked around the detective's broad shoulder so she could see me. "Hi, Mrs. Foxladle."

Worry leeched from her gaze when she spotted me and the automatic smile I was used to seeing made an appearance. "Naida. I'm surprised to see you here. Have you two decided to join book club?"

She slid a look from me to Grym and frowned. "Or did something happen at your beautiful store?"

Too late, I realized I'd be unable to explain my connection to the murders. Mrs. Foxladle was human, non-magic, and she only knew me as a bookstore owner. Any mention of magical artifacts would only earn me a confused look at best, and a suggestion to seek therapy at worst.

"I requested that Ms. Griffith accompany me, ma'am," Grym told her in a kind tone. "I know she's a friend of yours."

Though to my ears his explanation felt weak, it seemed to appease Mrs. Foxladle. "I see." She stepped back, opening the door wider. "Please, come in."

I entered ahead of Grym, and he gently closed the door behind us. I stood in the small foyer for a moment, glancing around at the pristine cleanliness of the cluttered space. Mrs. Foxladle had filled her home with beloved items in abundance. Knick knacks perched beside pictures and framed notes, no doubt from young relatives judging by the colorful stick figures adorning the careworn sheets of paper inside the frames.

Dated furniture took up much of the space in the living room. Stacks of books, newspapers, and magazines were piled high on every available flat surface.

"Please, sit. Make yourselves comfortable. Can I get you some tea? Muffins?"

"No!" Grym and I both exclaimed too quickly and a tiny bit too emphatically.

Mrs. F blinked under the force of our refusal.

I laughed self-consciously. "Sorry. We just had tea. But thanks so much for the offer."

Frowning slightly, Mrs. Foxladle lowered herself into a small upholstered chair, her hand falling as if by habit into a basket filled with balls of yarn beside the chair. She pulled out a work in progress, knitted in wide pink, white, and sky-blue stripes, and settled it into her lap without touching the needles stuck into the fluffy yarn. "What's happened?" she asked me, her gray gaze filled with worry.

Grym cleared his throat, drawing her attention to him. "Mrs. Foxladle, I'm afraid we have some bad news."

Her small, bent fingers tugged the knitting needles from her work and yanked gently on the ball of yarn inside the basket, wrapping the yarn around a needle and beginning to work. "Please just tell me, Detective. I can't abide dithering."

"We received a call from your friend, Celia Pepper's landlady tonight. She'd knocked on Celia's door, and it had opened under her knock. When she went inside the apartment to investigate..."

"She found Celia dead," Mrs. Foxladle said, nodding. Her small chin firmed, and her hands worked more rapidly over the striped object in her lap. "I knew it."

Grym glanced my way, eyes narrowing, and I gave him a quick shake of my head, having no idea what was going on.

"Ma'am, what do you mean when you say you knew it?" Grym asked her.

Mrs. Foxladle sighed. "I've been telling Celia that man was dangerous. She just wouldn't believe me."

Grym pulled his notebook from his pocket. "What man?"

But Mrs. Foxladle just kept knitting, her brow furrowed.

Grym looked at me again.

I leaned forward in my chair. "Mrs. Foxladle, Celia didn't die alone."

That brought her head snapping up. "*He* was with her?"

"No. The book club..." I said, my stomach twisting as I saw realization fill her gaze.

Her hands fell to her lap, the work forgotten. "No!"

I grasped one of her hands, finding it cold and soft. "I'm so sorry."

A single tear slipped from her eyes. "All of them?"

"I'm afraid so." My voice was gentle, my own eyes stinging from the sight of her pain. I'd met a couple of the other women in her book club. They'd been regulars at Croakies. Not as regular as Mrs. Foxladle, but regular enough that I'd had an easy relationship with them. Celia had always been a little stiff but friendly in an offhand way. Bonnie Witherspoon had been cheerful and kind.

Mrs. Foxladle swiped a hand over her cheeks, sniffling. "How?"

I looked at Grym. We couldn't tell her about the artifact. I wasn't even sure how Grym was going to handle it with his human superiors. There were really no bodies, and there was no way to prove foul play. Even the landlady had only reported a concern about the open door and empty apartment. She'd suspected something untoward had happened, but she didn't mention murder or even violence.

"They were poisoned," Grym told the elderly woman.

Mrs. Foxladle's hands returned to their work, her fingers moving rapidly through the stitches as tears slid down her cheeks.

"Mrs. Foxladle," Grym tried again, "Who is this man you mentioned?"

She shook her head. "I don't know. She met him online. He befriended her there." She sniffled angrily. "He was much younger than she was. I told her he was only after her money, but she wouldn't listen to me."

"Money?" I frowned. "Celia didn't seem like she had a lot of money," I offered before I thought about it. The woman had always been trying to get me to sell her brand-new books at a discount, and

I'd had my hands full dealing with her. She tended to get angry when I refused. She'd even gone so far as to damage the cover of a book once, declaring I had to sell it to her at a discount since it was damaged.

I'd just put the book on the shelf that morning. It had been in pristine condition. But there'd been no way for me to prove it, and I'd figured it wasn't worth losing a good customer, so I'd given her the discount she'd asked for. I realized that being frugal didn't necessarily speak to Celia's financial situation, but nothing in her life seemed to scream money to me. Her clothing had been old and well-worn. Her small car was in good shape but it was a small, very basic model, probably very inexpensive. And her apartment had been unassuming, in a part of town that wasn't known for its wealth.

"Celia was tight with a dollar," Mrs. Foxladle said, her lips pursing. "She pinched every penny until it squeaked."

"Did she keep a lot of money at home?"

Mrs. Foxladle glanced at Grym. "A few hundred dollars maybe."

He nodded. "Did she tell you anything about this man?"

"Only that he was very handsome. She lamented that she wasn't younger and prettier because she was afraid he'd lose interest."

"How long were they seeing each other?" I asked.

"Not long. I'd say they only went out a couple of times."

"Had he met any of the other ladies in your club?" Grym asked.

"Not that I know of." Her voice wobbled and she frowned over her knitting.

I wondered if it was starting to sink in that she'd lost five of her friends.

"What about the other ladies?" Grym asked.

Her head came up and her eyes filled with confusion. "What?"

"Did you know of anyone else who might have wanted to harm your friends?"

She seemed to melt right before my very eyes. Her hands stilled on the knitting, her shoulders drooped, and she collapsed in on herself. "I can't believe they're gone."

I squeezed her hand. "What can I do for you?"

She shook her head, reaching to snag a tissue from a small box on the table. "Nothing, hon. I just need some time. I'll need to contact Celia's son, and Bonnie's daughter. The others..." Her voice trailed off as she seemed to realize how much there was to do when you were the one left behind. She scrubbed a hand over her brow. "I need to tell their other friends what happened." She glanced up and gave me a tremulous smile. "Thank you for coming, hon. I appreciate hearing it from you."

Her dismissal was clear. I nodded, giving her

hand one last squeeze, and stood up. "If you need anything at all."

She patted my hand. "I'll call. I promise."

"Thank you for your help," Grym told the elderly woman. He reached down and took her hand, giving it a squeeze. "I'm going to do everything in my power to find the person responsible for this. You have my word."

She nodded, sniffling. "Thank you, young man."

We left, waiting to hear her engage the locks before stepping down onto the sidewalk. The night was quiet, the air moist from the earlier rain. The moon was lost behind a thick bank of charcoal-colored clouds and a shiver slid down my spine.

I rubbed my arms. "I feel so badly for her."

Grym sighed. "Telling the survivors is the worst part of my job." When I didn't respond, he dropped an arm around my shoulders, giving me a quick squeeze. "She's a very strong lady, Naida. The business of putting things in order will keep her on her feet until she remembers why getting on with life is important."

I sighed. "That's really the secret, isn't it? To life? When something knocks your legs out from under you, the hardest thing is remembering why you shouldn't just fold into a blubbering pile of remorse and sadness and give up."

He grimaced. "I wouldn't have put it quite that way...but yes. Basically."

I caught a movement out of the corner of one eye and turned as we reached Grym's dark sedan at the curb.

The street was empty, the long line of brick and stone buildings appeared shrouded in sadness. The shadows seemed filled with menace. Sorrow filled my chest, making it hard to breathe.

There were five women who were no longer enjoying books, tea, and each other. My gaze skimmed back toward Mrs. Foxladle's home. And one more who wouldn't enjoy those things for a while.

The soft sound of wings beat the air above me and I looked up to find an owl skating across the sky, its distinctive form made ominous by the thick gray background of storm clouds.

I shivered violently. For just a beat, panic had risen to choke off my breathing.

The owl reminded me too much of the Quilleran witch who'd nearly taken Lea and me down one dark night in the midst of another case.

Then I smiled at myself. Margot Quilleran was locked away, unable to hurt anybody. And the owl I'd seen above had been much too small to be her anyway.

I was letting my emotions rocket out of control, setting me off balance.

I climbed into Grym's car and buckled myself in as he pulled away from the curb.

"Do you want to go home? Or would you like to come with me to talk to the landlady? I want to ask her about this man Mrs. Foxladle mentioned."

"I'm in." What can I say? There was no way I was going to miss that.

3

IN SEARCH OF MOTOROIL

The manager of the *Enchanted Glenn Apartments* opened the Office door when Grym knocked, her long, thin face drooping downward like melted wax on a hot summer day. "Yes?"

Grym showed her his badge. "Ms. Wexille?"

"Yes. Is this about the missing resident in building four?"

"Can we come in, ma'am?" Grym asked firmly but politely.

I watched the woman carefully, noting the nervous slide of her gaze toward me and then back to Grym. "Who's that?"

"This is my associate, Ms. Griffith."

I offered her a smile. "Hi."

The wax around her eyes melted some more, giving her a hound dog look. "Can't we just talk right here?"

The way she kept glaring at me made me wonder what she thought I was going to do to her. I didn't think I looked like a contract killer who targeted apartment managers.

"If you'd be more comfortable, we can talk down at the station," he told the woman, his tone a little less polite and a little firmer.

She twitched, her lips melting downward at the corners. "No. That won't be necessary." She stepped away from the door, leaving it open a crack in reluctant invitation.

Grym and I shared a look, and he shook his head.

Following him inside, I stayed by the door, closing it behind us. Grym stood in front of the manager's desk, which took up most of the front living area. It was clearly an office-slash-living quarters for the woman. Aside from the oversized wooden desk, the room contained a couple of recliners and a super-sized television on a black glass stand. The walls had a few, unexceptional paintings that looked like they might have come from a doctor's office.

Ms. Wexille dropped wearily into her desk chair and indicated the chair across from her. "Sit, Detective. Tell me how I can help." Her tone made it sound less like she was offering help, and more like she was demanding to get it over with.

Grym didn't seem put off by her tone. He probably encountered it a lot. I waited until he'd begun questioning her about finding the book club women before sending a swirl of keeper energy through the space, just in case.

The pale brown gaze inside the melting skin caught on the ribbon of energy, watching it slide around the room, before skimming back to me with a glare.

Interesting.

Ms. Wexille wasn't human.

I met her glare with a smile and a shrug.

"Ms. Wexille, why did you go to Mrs. Pepper's apartment tonight?"

Still glaring at me, the manager shrugged. "She owed me for some repairs that had been done in her unit. I went to collect." She grimaced. "I guess I won't be getting reimbursed for those repairs now."

Nice, I thought. "Why do you say that?" I asked, curious. If the woman didn't know the book club ladies were dead, why would she make such a statement?

Wexille shrugged. "I'm just guessing she skipped town."

"Her phone and purse were still in the apartment," Grym told the woman. "There's no sign that she took any personal items with her."

I was a little surprised he was sharing that information, but I figured he was trying to catch her in a lie.

Wexille skimmed me a speculative look. "I didn't search the place."

"Tell me what happened when you arrived at Mrs. Pepper's home," Grym instructed. He sat back in his chair, arms crossed over his chest. He stared at the manager until she pulled her glare from me.

She shrugged. "I already told the other cop this."

"And I need you to tell me," Grym said, his tone cool.

She sighed. "I knocked on the door, and it swung open. I was surprised because Mrs. Pepper had always been a stickler for locking everything up. She acted like she was living in the projects or something."

"Go on," Grym said.

"I called out to her and nobody answered, so I walked inside. I kept calling her name, but nobody ever answered."

"Why did you call the police?" he asked.

"Something didn't feel right. The table looked as if they'd all left in a hurry. Given that and the open door, it felt like something bad had happened." Her gaze skimmed sideways, avoiding Grym's.

"And you say you weren't aware she'd left her phone and purse behind?"

"Of course not. Do you think I searched her bedroom?" The woman snorted. "I hurried out of there and called the police."

Grym stared at her for a long moment. When he

spoke again, his tone was soft, cold. "How did you know her purse and cell were in her bedroom if you didn't look for them?"

She blinked, all the color leeching from her long, melting face. "I...um..." She frowned. "Okay, I did look in the bedroom, but just because I wanted to make sure she wasn't in there."

He held her gaze, his expression hot enough to burn.

My brain formed a picture of the heat melting the wax and her face rolling off her skull and plopping onto the desk.

"It's the strangest thing," Grym finally told her. "There wasn't a single bill in her wallet. Nothing. No money whatsoever."

Wexille blinked rapidly, shifting in her chair.

"When we check that wallet for fingerprints, we aren't going to find yours, are we Ms. Wexille?"

The woman's head shook back and forth so hard the droopy skin wobbled on the air. "I didn't steal anything from that woman, Detective. And you can't prove I did."

No, I thought. She was probably right. I was pretty sure her fingertips were made of wax. They'd probably melted together under the intensity of her larceny decades ago.

Grym sat looking down at his hands for a long moment, and then lifted an intense gaze toward the woman sitting across the desk. "Let's set the discussion about Mrs. Pepper's personal effects aside for the moment..."

I nearly smiled. His implication was that they'd be revisiting the subject, leaving the landlady to decide if she wanted to earn herself some goodwill by cooperating or not.

She narrowed her gaze on him, her lips a thin line on her droopy face.

"What can you tell me about Mrs. Pepper's personal life?"

The woman blinked in surprise. "Personal? How would I know? We weren't friends."

Thank goodness for that, I thought. Since she'd most likely stolen money from the poor woman after she was murdered.

"Don't sell yourself short," Grym told her with a smile. "You're aware of everything that happens in this complex. Aren't you?"

Ms. Wexille frowned, eyeing him like she would a particularly hairy spider, and then nodded. "It's my job to know what's going on."

"Right. And you take pride in that job. Don't you?"

She shrugged, still looking at him like she knew what he was up to, but unwilling to call him on it just in case he was really complimenting her as he pretended.

"Tell me who visited Mrs. Pepper on a regular basis."

Wexille twined her fingers together on top of her messy desk and leaned forward. "Those annoying women were there every Tuesday night. I've had to ask them not to park in the residents' spots several times." She shook her head, disgusted.

"Did they ever come over on other nights? Or during the day?"

"Not that I know of," Ms. Wexille said.

"Who else came regularly?"

The manager turned sly. "Him. That's who you're wondering about, isn't it?"

Grym's expression didn't change. "Him?"

"The handsome one. I thought he was her grandson, but Pepper was all over the place bragging about her new boyfriend." Ms. Wexille's lips curled in disgust. "He was thirty years younger than her if he was a day."

"Did she give you a name?" I asked, earning myself a frown from the cop. I fought a shrug. He'd asked me to come along.

"Yeah. It was something strange." She tapped a ragged nailed finger against her lips. "What was it..."

We waited for a moment and then she shook her head, giving Grym a coy look. "Nope. I can't remember."

He nodded. "Maybe a trip downtown to talk about the missing money from Pepper's purse would jog your memory."

"Motoroil." She pretended joy at the word. "See, I told you it was strange."

"His name was Motoroil?" Grym asked, clearly not believing her.

"I swear, that was the name. That old woman just beamed when she talked about him."

"Did you ever meet him face-to-face?" I asked.

"Nah. I saw him get out of his car once and walk to the door. He was a strappin' young thing with dark hair. That's all I could see from where I was."

"What kind of car did he drive?" Grym asked.

"It was white, kind of boxy."

Grym seemed to be waiting for her to elaborate.

"That's all I've got for you." She stood up. "Now, if you'll excuse me, I'm a busy woman."

Grym stood slowly. "Thanks for your time, Ms. Wexille."

She ignored him, staring at me. "You're the KoA."

It wasn't a question. She had clearly recognized my magic. "I am."

My response brought a frown. "You think a rogue artifact did this?"

Grym vibrated with curiosity but stayed silent, letting me run with the potentially enlightening line of questioning. "It's one option. That's why Detective Grym invited me along today."

Wexille nodded, looking thoughtful. "Pepper was human. There was no magic in her. I can't speak for the other ladies though."

"What about the man..." My lips quivered. "Motoroil?"

"He could have been supernormal, I guess. He was definitely a good salesman, I know that."

"Salesman?" I asked. "What do you mean?"

"He always carried a bag with him when he came, a black leather one. I'd seen him loading it up with jars of some kind of white cream before he went into Pepper's place. I figured him for a salesman of some kind. That's why I was so surprised when she called him her boyfriend."

"Do you know if he sold stuff to anybody else in the complex?" Grym asked.

She shrugged, her gaze locked on mine. "I lost a friend to a rogue artifact, once. If I hear anything, I'll let you know."

I inclined my chin. "Thank you. I'd appreciate it."

4

IT'S SO HARD TO GET GOOD STAFF
THESE DAYS!

To say that chaos had descended on Croakies while I was gone would be too gentle a statement. What I walked into was well beyond chaos, bordering on apocalyptic. And I'm sorry to say that my usually competent assistant wasn't handling it at all well.

I opened the door and stepped inside the store, looking up at the strident clang of the bell above my head.

The bell usually gave off a soft tinkle. A pleasant sound meant to warn me when someone came into the shop. Nothing like the screechy clang I'd just been greeted with.

I was reaching for the charred and dented mash of metal, my thoughts roiling in search of an explanation, when Sebille screamed at me. "Duck!"

Sebille's usually calm and snotty tone was

neither calm nor snotty. In fact, it sounded panicked, and it startled me into reacting immediately.

I ducked.

A silvery bolt of energy burned through the air right above my head, sizzling against a wayward, wind-blown strand and leaving behind the sour stench of burning hair. The bolt of energy slammed into the door, etching a char mark into the heavy wood and pinging harmlessly away.

"Dervish dimples, Sebille! What in the universe is going on?" Hitting my knees, I reached back and locked the door so no unsuspecting customers could come through.

My assistant made a strangled sound, and I jerked my gaze toward the dividing door between the bookstore and the artifact library in the back.

Sebille's slender form was framed in the open doorway, her striped-sock-clad legs spread to press against either side in a clear attempt to keep her from being propelled forward. She'd flung one arm to the side and had a death grip on the frame.

Her freckled face was pinched, her pointed ears red enough to match her fiery hair, and her shimmering green eyes looked ready to pop out of her face. "This thing's out of control..." she managed to pant out, her arm shooting into the air and sending another silvery bolt of energy into the bookstore ceiling.

Plaster dust sifted onto my head, the ceiling

broken and scorched from the destructive magic. Chunks of glowing embers sizzled where the magic had sheared off a chunk of the wood beneath the surface.

The object clutched in Sebille's hand spit sparks and emitted a high-pitched buzz like a dying hive of demon bees. A green orb was anchored into the tip of the staff by a twisting maze of black metal and thorn branches. It glowed brightly, pulsing in time to Sebille's own green orbs.

Oh, oh.

I shoved to my feet and started toward her. "Troll boogers, Sebille. What are you doing with Maleficent's staff?" The staff swung in my direction, and I barely managed to dive out of the way before the magic arrow it threw seared a path toward the wall behind me. The explosion sent chunks of drywall into the air in a shower of debris that thumped down all over the floor, the books, and me.

"You need to drop it, Sebille!" I screamed.

She gritted her teeth and shook her head. "I can't," she hissed out. "It's trying to escape."

The staff re-aimed itself toward the ceiling and sent two barrels of energy into the light fixture, exploding it into a blizzard of falling pieces. Tiny shards of glass rained down, peppering me with painful stabs and burning abrasions as they fell.

The staff shot downward again, fighting Sebille to focus its bile on me. I felt my eyes go wide. "Um,

Sebille." I stepped sideways, and the staff followed me. "Sebille!"

"I...can't..." Her face was purple with strain. She let go of the doorframe and used both hands to clutch the staff. Her upper body swayed forward, tugged by the artifact into the room. Only her feet braced against the framing kept her from flying right at me with the staff at the helm.

I looked at the sales counter, trying to judge if I could make it behind the barrier before the staff fired at me.

It would be close. But other than that, all I had were the bookshelves. I really didn't want the stupid thing blowing up my books.

Then movement caught my eye and I turned, horrified to see Mr. Slimy hop out from between the shelves, black eyes bulging. He stopped and looked at me, his throat pulsing as he sized me up.

"Naida!"

My gaze jerked around and horror sliced through me, turning my gut to mush. "No!"

The staff was pointed at Mr. Slimy, the green orb pulsing with power it was about to fire into the unsuspecting frog.

I made a sudden decision. The only one I could make under the circumstances. Mr. Slimy wasn't just a frog. He was Mr. Wicked's best friend, and the current fleshy home of my friend, the ghost witch.

Besides, if I was willing to admit it to myself, I was kind of fond of the little guy.

My feet were moving before I could think about what I was doing. I ran directly at Sebille, praying to the goddess that the staff wouldn't sense me coming and fire a warning shot.

Sebille's eyes widened, and she started to shake her head.

Energy spat from the tip of the staff.

I launched myself off the ground.

Energy boiled from the orb and hung in the air, roiling for a beat as it focused on its target.

I hit the staff from the side, shoving it away as the energy exploded and hit the end of my longest book-shelf, turning it to kindling when it struck.

Sebille cried out and fell backward, slamming against the edge of the door. She slid down as the staff hung in the air, spun in a circle, and went upright, shooting toward the picture window. The rogue artifact crashed right through the glass, disap-pearing into the darkness in a fiery trail.

More glass blasted into the room, sucked inward by the magic wards Croakies was saturated with, and turning the bookstore into a cornucopia of pain and destruction. I ducked, covering my head and praying the frog would have the sense to take cover. As the tiny splinters of glass and hunks of paper from the shredded books rained down on us, I looked at Sebille. "Are you okay?"

She blew paper off her face, grimacing. "Mostly." She held her hands out and looked at her blackened palms, wincing. "Ouch."

I hurried over and made her show me her palms. "Ouch is right. Can you heal them?"

Sebille shook her head. "My energy won't heal this damage. The staff's magic is blocking me somehow."

"I can take you to your mother."

Queen Sindra, Sebille's mother and queen of the Fae in Enchanted, lived in the lot behind Croakies, inside my friend Lea's massive greenhouse.

Sebille shook her head again. "She's gone to Illusion City to talk to the Council about relocating to the Illusory Forest."

The Fae's home, dubbed Toadstool City, had been burned to the ground in magical fire as retribution for their rescuing a litter of enchanted kittens from a local witch family. The Quillerans had been using the poor babies for dark purposes.

Lea had kindly offered to let the Fae live in her own private ecosystem out behind both our shops. I'd thought it had been a mutually satisfactory solution, which was why I was both unhappy and surprised to hear the queen was seeking out other living options.

Frowning, I pushed to my feet. "I'll go get the first aid kit."

Florence Nightingale's first aid kit had disappeared after her death in 1910 and had recently been unearthed during refurbishing of her family home, Embley Park, in Wellow Hampshire. I'd been called to travel to the beautiful home to retrieve the first aid kit. Now the location of Hampshire Collegiate School, Embley Park was every bit as beautiful in its current state as I imagined it had been when Florence had been alive. I'd been keeping the magical healing kit in a handy spot on a low shelf in the artifact library. Just in case.

The kit was a powerful artifact whose constantly renewing salves and wrappings could heal a multitude of non-life-threatening wounds within seconds. Even, hopefully, magical burns from one of my most dangerous artifacts. Which, unhappily, now seemed to be flying around Enchanted unchained and with a green-orb-sized chip on its shoulder.

My mind boiling with questions, I grabbed the unassuming metal box with a dented and chipped depiction of the *Rod of Asclepius* on its worn front surface and headed back out front. Maleficent's staff had been safely locked into the toxic magic vault when I'd left Croakies a few hours ago. "What on earth were you thinking, Sebille?" I asked as I knelt beside her.

"It's not my fault, Naida," she said with a return of her snotty tone. "I just opened the door a crack and the thing shot through. I barely caught it before it escaped into the bookstore."

"What was the dividing door doing open, anyway?" Opening the box, I pulled out a small glass jar and tugged the stopper free. I dipped my finger into the yellow-tinged salve inside and rubbed it over Sebille's blackened and blistered palms.

Sebille shrugged. "Ask the frog, he and your annoying cat probably opened it."

Given that Mr. Slimy was out of his terrarium, that did seem likely. For some reason, Mr. Wicked didn't like Mr. Slimy's new home and took every opportunity to rescue him from the glass tank.

I wasn't exactly sure *how* he was rescuing the frog, I hadn't seen him do it, but my cat had wondrous and magical ways of doing things that constantly defied logic and magical knowledge.

I glanced around. "Where is said, naughty feline now?"

"No idea. Probably denting your pillow upstairs. I don't doubt he's taken himself away from the scene of destruction for the sake of plausible deniability." Sebille hissed as the magic started to work, her skin bubbling beneath the powerful healing magics.

I finished coating both palms and then wrapped them in the tattered gauze, winding the dingy cloth around and around her hand several times and then encircling her thumbs and ripping to tie it off.

As I re-stoppered the small bottle and dropped it and the remaining gauze back into the box, the items replenished themselves with a spark of magic.

"That should do it," I told my assistant as I stood. I eyed her when she didn't respond. "Are you okay?"

Sebille's face was pale under the pain of the repair going on beneath the gauze. Sweat coated her brow and darkened the roots of her bright hair. "I've been better."

I reached down and helped her stand, taking care to avoid her wrapped hands. "You should rest. When you wake up, your hands will probably be healed."

She nodded, though I saw the worry in her gaze. "Here..." I pulled a smaller bottle from the kit, eyeing the dark brown glass and giving it a little shake to check the liquid inside. "Once you're on the couch, put two drops of this on your tongue and stopper it immediately. It's magical Laudanum and will knock you on your keister in seconds once you've taken it. You'll sleep for a couple of hours."

She clasped the bottle gingerly between her bandaged fingers. "I don't want to leave you to clean up this mess alone."

I smiled. "It will be fine." I gave her a wink. "I have Cinderella's wand, remember?"

Her smile widened. We'd only just liberated the wand from a used toy store in Enchanted the day before. I'd been forced to grab the sparkly pink wand out of the hand of an adorable toddler girl as her mother glared at me. I'd felt really bad about that. The child had been inconsolable, and Sebille's grumpy face jutting toward the screaming little girl hadn't helped.

"I want to use it!" Sebille whined, sounding more like that toddler than she'd like to realize.

"I'll save some of the mess for you to clean," I promised, grinning. Unlike the evil staff, which had almost made a crime scene out of my cozy little bookstore, Cinderella's wand was basically harmless, good only for tidying up and restoring things to the way they'd been.

I closed the door behind Sebille and turned to look at the mess, sighing.

Even with the wand, it was going to take me a while to clean it up. As my gaze slipped over the glass-covered carpet near the bookshelves, I thought of Mr. Slimy.

"Oh!" I hurried over to the spot where he'd been when the staff had fired, dropping to my knees before thinking. Pain sliced through my knees in multiple spots. "Ouch! Frog spectacles!" I went back to my toes and carefully looked underneath the bottom shelf. "Mr. Slimy?"

Thump.

The sound came from farther down the shelf. I moved around to the aisle between the tall shelves, finding it relatively clear of debris. I hit the ground again, my gaze scouring the dusty shadows beneath the shelf. "Mr. Slimy, are you under here?"

Thump. Thump. Thumpity-thump.

That would be a resounding, yes. I finally found his glassy-eyed stare peering at me from the spot where the two shelves were pressed together. He was huddling under the squared-off archway made by the legs as if hunkering down for an earthquake.

"Come here, you little green booger."

I reached for the squishy green interloper and he hopped, his head smacking into the underside of the shelf.

Thump.

"Stop that, you're going to give yourself brain damage." I thought about that for a minute and then grinned. "Oh yeah, that would assume you had a brain."

Thumpthumpthumpity-thump.

I lunged toward the concussion-seeking amphibian, falling on my face as he somehow dodged away from my grip. "Argh!!!"

Thump. Thump. Thump! I narrowed my gaze. The frog wasn't moving but the thumping was still happening.

Thumpthumpthump!

I sat up and stared at the exterior door. Someone was pounding on it.

Caterpillar cankles! I'd forgotten to put up the *Closed* sign.

I hurried over and peered through the broken picture window, seeing a woman who looked to be in her early sixties standing outside. The woman had graying blonde hair, cut into a cute pixie style, and beautiful green eyes. She seemed more upset than being thwarted from buying a cat cozy mystery should inspire.

I unlocked the door, opening it a crack and smiling out at my nervous customer. "I'm sorry, we're closed."

Her frown wrinkles deepened. "I really need to speak with you, Naida. It's important."

I finally recognized the woman. Her name was Franny Clauss. And then my eyes went wide. Franny was one of Mrs. Foxladle's book club friends. I'd only met her once or twice but seeing her at my door, after what had happened at book club, finally jogged my memory.

I yanked the door open. "Franny, are you okay?" Even if she was, she was about to not be so okay when I told her four, apparently not five as we'd suspected, of her friends were dead.

She shook her head. "Not even close. Please, can I come inside?" She glanced worriedly over her shoulder like she was afraid she was being followed. "Please?" she asked again when I hesitated.

I opened the door wider. "Okay. But please be careful. We've had an...accident."

Franny gave the train wreck of my store a cursory once-over and frowned. "You weren't kidding about the accident." She settled an oversized leather bag to the floor, looking around with a shocked expression.

I nodded, sighing as I relocked the door and turned off my *Open* sign. I flipped the cardboard sign hanging from the door to *Closed* and turned to her. "We thought you were dead."

The words flew from my lips before I could stop them. As soon as they hit the space between us, I realized how they'd sounded. "I'm sorry..."

Franny shook her head. "Don't be. That's why I'm here." Tears filled her gaze and slid down her pasty white cheeks. "I saw you and that Detective at Celia's today. I know you're a keeper. I needed to talk to you about what happened."

I blinked in surprise. "You know I'm a Keeper of the Artifacts?" I hated to be repetitive, but I needed to verify what she was telling me. There could be no misunderstandings. Once we engaged in the conversation I knew we were about to have, there was no turning back.

Franny's gaze slid around the space. "Does this mess have anything to do with the staff I saw fly out of here a few minutes ago?" She pointed to the front window with its perfect round hole.

"Yes. I'm afraid Maleficent's staff got the better of my assistant."

Franny frowned. "That's not good."

As understatements went, that one was the equivalent of painting an elephant's toenails with a fairy's toothbrush. "No, it certainly isn't."

"I only wish it was the most dangerous artifact

out there. But I'm afraid it's not. At least you see this one coming," she said, wringing her hands together.

My pulse picked up at her words. "Tell me what happened to your friends," I urged gently.

"I wish I knew!" Her response hadn't been what I was expecting. "I came late and called out to them as I hurried through the apartment, heading to the restroom." She flushed. "I'd had a really large coffee on my way over. It hit me hard."

"What happened then?"

"I waved at them as I hurried past and they laughed..."

"So they were all, okay?" I asked.

"Yes. Smiling, talking about this week's book, and drinking tea."

"Okay. Go on."

"Celia called out that she had a surprise for us and told me to hurry."

"I didn't even respond." Fresh tears slipped down her face. "I had to pee so badly. By the time I came back out, they were gone."

Poor woman, she was feeling guilty for answering a normal call of nature. At least she hadn't had to sing the *Make Me a Magic Muffin Mister* song to flush, or she might have taken even longer to get back to her friends. "You couldn't have known," I told her, reaching out to clasp her icy hand.

"I was only in there a couple of minutes. I'll admit I could have gone faster. I was..." Her cheeks pinkened. "Celia has a vast number of toiletries. She's always been big on natural cosmetics and stuff. Really expensive makeup. She gets a lot of samples to try. I can't afford that type of thing, so I check hers out whenever I'm there."

"Did you use any of it?"

The pink in her cheeks deepened. "I did. I'm so sorry."

"What did you use?"

"Just some hand lotion. It's got pig placenta in it, and it's supposed to be a really good anti-aging cream. It sounds terrible, but it smells like roses. It's really very nice."

"You suffered no effects from the cream?"

"Well, no. Except my hands are really soft." She frowned. "You think some kind of cosmetic did this?"

"Possibly. Do you think your friends did the same as you? Trying Celia's samples?"

She nodded enthusiastically, seeming to find some relief from the guilt in the knowledge that she wasn't alone in her curiosity. "Celia didn't mind. She encouraged us to try the stuff. I think she got a kickback if she helped sell some of it."

I nodded, thinking about what Franny had told me. If everyone at the table tried the same thing, it was possible something in Celia's collection of cosmetics killed them all. Although the timing would have to be perfect, and that seemed unlikely. Still, I'd tell Grym what I'd learned. He'd been planning on having everything on the table tested for poison, he might want to test the stuff in the bathroom too.

Franny was staring at her hands, her shoulders drooping and tears flowing freely down her cheeks. I couldn't imagine how she felt. In addition to raw grief, she was probably dealing with a combination of survivor's guilt and just plain relief she'd somehow escaped her friends' fate.

"Do you know where Celia got her samples?" I asked, my question tugging her from her thoughts.

Franny shook her head. "I don't, I'm sorry. I just couldn't afford to buy that type of thing myself, so I didn't pay much attention to her when she talked about them."

"The landlady said Celia had a new boyfriend. Had you met him?"

Franny looked surprised. "She did? No. I had no idea. What was he like? Was he younger?" Franny frowned. "Celia was always trying to attract younger men. I think it's one of the reasons she spent so much on anti-aging cosmetics."

Parakeet pants! I'd really been hoping Franny would be able to dish the dirt on the new heartthrob. Something told me he was up to his boy toy eyebrows in the women's deaths.

But one thing was still bothering me. "How did you know they...um...?"

"How'd I know they were dead?"

Franny's red-rimmed eyes overflowed with a fresh batch of tears. "I was shocked to see them all gone. I walked over to the table and looked at it, seeing the untasted tea and food. The chairs hadn't even been pulled away from the table like they would be if they'd gotten up. I called out to them, but nobody answered. Then I heard a cry and glanced under the table."

She held a hand in front of her face. It shook violently as all the color ran from her face at the memory. "It was horrible."

I could only imagine. She must have seen them in a condition that was prior to the final embryo state. It would be something that would stick with her for the rest of her life.

I reached out and pulled her into a hug as she broke down completely, holding her until the sobbing stopped and the violent trembling lessened.

Then I told her Mrs. Foxladle was alive. It was the only good news in the whole mess.

Thank heavens, the two women could console each other in their mutual grief.

5

MOONLIGHT MAGIC

*R*ustin oozed into view as I closed the door behind Franny Clauss. He hovered above the floor, his handsome face pinched and his gaze behind the wire-rimmed glasses all judgy.

I glared at him. "It's not my fault."

He jerked his head toward the thumping underneath the bookshelves. "Is it your fault my frog bus is currently giving himself a concussion?"

"No." I sighed. "I tried to get him out of there, but some of *you* must be infusing his little amphibian brain. He was being difficult."

Rustin sighed, extending a hand toward the shadowed space.

A beat later, the frog slid out from under the shelf and levitated into its glass house.

"Ribbit!" Slimy said in apparent thanks.

I frowned at the ghost witch. "I see your powers are getting stronger."

He shrugged.

"Any chance you're the one who put him on the floor in the first place?"

Rustin's arms were crossed over his chest again, his gaze locked on me along the length of his perfect nose. "Why on earth would I do that?"

He wouldn't. Rustin had more at stake in keeping Mr. Slimy whole and healthy than anybody. Slimy might be bored inside his glass prison, but he was safe.

I watched the squishy green critter hop into the little pond I'd made him and smiled. Then I narrowed my gaze. *Did his head look flatter than it had before?*

Yikes!

My phone rang, and I hit *Answer* without looking. "Croakies Book Store."

There was a long pause, and then a screechy voice with a snotty undertone filled the silence. "Naida Keeper, are you responsible for the magical staff blasting its way through Enchanted at this moment?"

I frowned. "Who is this?" There was no way I was owning up to that disaster unless I was forced to.

"This is your conscience speaking."

My frown deepened. I was pretty sure I recognized the screech *and* the snot. "Is that you, Rasputin?"

"Maybe," he responded, a caw rounding off the single word.

"Why are you calling me?" I asked the bossy raven familiar of a fourth-generation witch named Quilleran.

"Maddie told me to call you in her professional capacity as PTB. You need to corral that artifact before it hurts someone."

The Powers That Be managed the magical world for the Universe, much as I managed the magical artifacts.

Well...since one of my artifacts was currently running rogue around Enchanted...I kind of hoped she managed her charges better than I did.

"A rogue staff? How did that happen?" I asked in as innocent a voice as I could muster. "Why am I just now hearing about this?"

"Nice try, Keeper. Maddie says to clean up your mess, or she'll have to come down there and do it herself."

I disconnected on a sigh. I'd had visions of sugar plums in the form of my nice soft pillow dancing in my head. Instead, I had to hit the streets and find a bratty staff with authority issues.

"Would you like some help?" Rustin asked.

I glanced at him in surprise. His face was still fixed in an arrogant expression, but his eyes looked hopeful. He was bored. I didn't blame him, Rustin was a smart and powerful witch. It had to be spectacularly boring to ride around inside a thought-challenged amphibian all day. Fortunately for everyone involved, along with helping him strengthen his powers in his new state of being, his Aunt Madeline had also figured out a way to extend the sphere of influence between Rustin and the frog, so we didn't need to carry Slimy around with us everywhere we went. As long as Rustin stayed within the Enchanted city limits he could be his own...erm...man.

"Sure. I can use all the help I can get," I told the ghost witch.

Rustin's expression didn't change, but light filled his gaze. "Great. I'll just pop into the artifact room for the Book of Pages."

Fortunately Rustin, who'd given me the book in the first place, could still work the book even from his wispy state, using the power of his mind to select a magical option from the book and set it into motion with his energy alone.

Mostly, so far, he'd just used that energy to shrink the book into a size I could put in my pocket, but that was helpful enough to make my life easier.

I'd grown kind of dependent on that book.

You aren't really going to leave me in here, are you? someone asked, inside my head.

I twitched in surprise, looking around for the voice I'd heard.

Slimy sat in his tiny pond, his eyes staring blankly ahead and his throat working over a series of mindless, ribbits.

Motion near the cabinet had me glancing that way. My cat, Mr. Wicked, jumped up onto the counter and folded his tail around his sleek form.

I blinked as I realized how big he'd gotten over the last weeks. He no longer looked like a kitten. That made me kind of sad.

"Are you talking to me, little man?" I asked, walking over and scooping him into my arms to give him a kiss between the ears. "Where have you been all day?"

His response was to purr loudly, rubbing his soft head under my chin.

Rustin reappeared in a flash of energized mist. "Ready?" he asked.

I nodded. "You want to come with?" I asked my cat, staring at him for a long moment.

"Are you expecting him to answer?" Rustin asked, his lips curved into a derisive grin.

Actually, I had been. "No. Of course not. Cats don't talk."

Wicked gave my chin a tiny nip, and I lowered him to the ground. "Okay. Let's go," I said.

My gaze slid over the mess in the store as we made our way to the door. I grumbled. It looked like

Sebille was going to get a chance to play with Cinderella's wand after all.

I reached for the door as Wicked scampered through behind Rustin.

Hesitating before closing the door, I fixed Slimy with a speculative look. "I'll bring some bugs back Mr. Slimy. I promise."

Joy of joys, a sarcastic voice said as I closed the door.

I glowered at Rustin, the smug grin on his face telling me he was messing with me again. "I'm not sure I'm going to enjoy having you get some of your magic back," I told him.

His only response was to bark out a laugh, clearly not worried about what I enjoyed or didn't.

"How are we going to find this thing?" Rustin asked as I pulled away from the curb in my little car.

I glanced his way. "I'm going to go to Enchanted Park and send out my sensing magic."

He frowned. "Why there?"

"The gazebo represents the exact center of the city."

"I did not know that."

I grinned across the short space between us. "Stick with me and you'll learn all kinds of stuff."

Rustin's chuckle was filled with warmth, his handsome face was relaxed, even happy. As I drove down the mostly deserted streets of the city, the street lights flashed patterns over the glass of his wire-rimmed spectacles.

I was happy to see him looking so relaxed. He'd had a rough few months since his horrible family put the whammy on him, giving him a bad case of frog butt.

"How are Madeline and Maude doing on the research?"

He shrugged, his expression tightening slightly. I immediately felt guilty for stealing a bit of his happiness from him and wished I could take my question back.

"They haven't figured out how to separate me completely from the frog yet, obviously. But they're extracting me in bits and pieces."

I grimaced, making the turn into the park. "Ew. I'm not going to wake up one morning to find your feet walking around Croakies without your body, am I?"

He laughed again, the new tension leeching from his form. "I'm speaking magically. The physical piece, once they finish the prep work, should be reasonably simple to accomplish."

I doubted any of what his aunt and cousin were attempting would be simple. But I didn't say what I was thinking. He probably didn't believe it would be that easy either.

I was happy to leave him with his delusions for the time being. I felt fairly certain Madeline and Maude Quilleran would eventually reverse the damage Rustin's Uncle had wrought.

Jacob Quilleran had been a formidable witch, but his sister was at least as formidable and probably a bit more so.

We wound our way through the heavily-treed park, navigating the winding but smoothly paved road by the light of a nearly full moon and my headlights. There were no streetlights in the belly of Enchanted Park, only a sky filled with silvery stars and the bloated silver-gold moon hanging overhead.

I pulled into a small parking lot and killed the engine, my headlights casting an intrusive wash of light over the pretty white framing of the delicate gazebo.

I'd spent many a happy day escaping the hot sun or a deluge of rain under the protective roofline of that gazebo. Growing up, visiting the Enchanted Park gazebo for picnics and magical rejuvenation had been a favorite outing.

I hadn't known that the special shape and location of the gazebo gave it magical properties that replenished spent magical energy.

I'd never visited the park at night.

Common sense told me it would be exactly the

same, only darker. But the fact that the pretty little gazebo was surrounded by dense tree growth, shadows pulsing just beyond the small well-kept lawn that encircled it like a protective moat, made it an entirely unique, even discomfiting experience.

Mr. Wicked jumped up from where he'd been curled in my lap and batted at a flying bug beating itself against the window. Watching him, I had to grin that I'd thought he'd been talking to me earlier. He was just a goofy cat that I loved more than anything. A goofy, magically-talented cat with mad skills. But he was still a cat.

When I didn't make a move to get out of my car, Rustin glanced my way. "Is there something wrong?"

I shook my head. "No. I've just never experienced it at night."

"Ah." He smiled. "Well, then you've been missing out. Come on, let me show you."

He disappeared from the seat and reappeared outside.

I gave a sigh, wrenching my door open and stepping out into the night. Mr. Wicked jumped out too, disappearing across the grass with his tail snapping the moist air. He was a kitty with a mission. I said a silent prayer to the goddess that legions of crickets wouldn't suffer violent deaths as a result of that mission.

I stood in the gravel looking around for a moment, the scent of ozone making my nose itch, and the soft touch of a moist breeze confirming an imminent storm.

The familiar sound of chirping from thousands of crickets filled the area around the structure, the rustle of leaves high above my head serving as the soundtrack to the insects' joyful melody. I pulled in a deep breath, closing my eyes and letting the natural music settle over me.

"Naida?"

My eyes popped open. I searched the area for the ghost witch, finding him standing under the gazebo, his form painted by prancing silver lights.

I smiled at the pretty picture. "Fairy lights?"

He shook his head, pointing toward the fat moon. "Special markings on the top and sides transform the moonlight into dancing light."

I stepped under with him, gasping with pleasure as the lights pirouetted over me, leaving behind little spurts of happy energy wherever they touched. I held my arms out to my sides and tilted my head back so the lights could bathe my face in the energizing glow. "It feels like a magical massage."

He nodded, grinning widely. "I've spent many a night under this gazebo, letting it heal the regrets and challenges of my life." Despite his obvious joy, his words made him frown. I knew he had trouble dealing with the fact that most of his family were evil. I also suspected he battled the tendency toward being ruthless himself.

I hadn't trusted him when we'd first met, despite feeling bad for him in his current circumstance, but I'd grown to understand Rustin better over the months since he'd been in my life, and I'd come to the conclusion that he was more like Maude and Madeline than he was Jacob. "Your choices are your own," I told him. "as are your mistakes. You don't need to carry the weight of your family's sins on your own shoulders."

Something soft and warm bounced against my calf. I looked down to find Mr. Wicked chasing the dancing illumination. He leaped straight up in the air and twisted, his claws extended as he swiped a paw through the pretty bursts of light. The light segmented into several ribbons of illumination where before there'd been only one.

"Look at that," I told Rustin, laughing. "Wicked changed the light with his claws. He's so special."

Rustin laughed too. "He's special, all right." Watching my cat tear across the gazebo and then slam on the brakes, sliding sideways several inches before shooting straight up into the air again when a particularly robust dancing light flared past him, Rustin added. "A special kind of crazy."

I shook my head.

"Let's get this show on the road," Rustin said after another moment.

I tugged on my seeking magic and it surged forward, exploding from my fingertips with more power than I'd ever experienced. I stumbled back from the force of it and laughed as a dozen thick gray ribbons of power emerged from my fingertips and shot out of the gazebo, traveling in every direction.

"Um, yeah..." Rustin said, looking sheepish. "I forgot to tell you about that. The energy under this roof adds oomph to your magic too."

"Let's hope it works more quickly than usual too," I said. "I've got a mess to clean up at home. I'd like to get this wrapped up fast."

Rustin nodded.

A distant chime sounded, carried on the moisture filling the air as the first rumble of thunder growled across the sky.

"And before it starts raining cats and frogs," I added.

Lightning flashed in the distance, a flash of yellow light that illuminated the outline of a large bird heading our way.

I tensed, my mind replaying the night Lea and I had battled the massive predator owl that had been Margot Quilleran in her shifted form. I reached over and tried to grasp Rustin's arm, but my hand found only cool energy.

"What is it?" he asked.

"Is that...?" Lighting flashed again and the owl was gone. But something else boiled at the edges of the dense tree line. I suddenly wished I'd brought Blackbeard's sword with me.

Silvery light flashed through the trees, followed by the sound of grunts and growls and something slashing through the underbrush.

I tensed, realizing I might have unleashed something I wasn't prepared to handle. I glanced at Rustin. "What's happening?"

Light flared across his glasses as he shrugged. "Whatever it is, it doesn't sound good."

Silvery balls of energy erupted around his hands, the energy spitting angrily as it grew. The ghost witch's handsome face showed tension, and his form became more solid as he tugged more magic forward.

Something bit at my fingers. I looked down to find my own magic swirling around my fists. My eyes went wide. I'd never been able to draw so much defensive energy. As a Sorceress, my powers generally ran to finding and wrangling artifacts. I had little to no defensive energy to call. But as I lifted my hands, looking in wonder at the power swirling there, I realized my meager stores were being amplified.

"It's the gazebo," Rustin told me. I turned to find him looking at my hands. "It's enhancing our gifts." He looked down at his nearly solid form. A wistful look filled his gaze. "It's making me solid again."

I opened my mouth to reassure him that Madeline would find a way to make him solid for good again, but the chaos building inside the trees chose that moment to burst forth, driving a slavering, red-eyed army of creatures from the woods. I couldn't believe my eyes when I saw...

Bunnies?

Rustin and I stared at the clearly hostile but huggable creatures, our gazes narrowing as they growled and hissed, their long, soft-looking ears dancing with rage.

"Um...Rustin..." I said, hoping he could tell me I was seeing things. "Please tell me we don't have to fry up a bunch of adorable bunnies tonight."

He sighed. "Maybe they'll settle down."

Judging by the way their delightful little faces scrunched in rage while emitting the most horrible growling sounds, I highly doubted it.

The shadows shifted again, and a few dozen more critters spilled out into the moonlight. Their nearly black eyes reflected the silvery light of the fat orb high above their heads. They lifted tiny paws with scary sharp claws as they stood on their hind legs and chattered aggressively.

Rustin's gaze swung to mine. "Squirrels? Really?"

Light slashed through the trees again. A loud bellowing made me jump and twitch, which caused me to send an errant flash of energy into the floor-boards, sheering off the tip of my shoe in the process. Sizzling pain shot through my foot as I apparently clipped a toe.

"Ouch, ouch, ouch..." I hopped around on one foot, falling backward in shock as several huge, golden forms broke from the trees, eyes blazing and brandishing massive antlers.

Deer.

The center buck threw back his head on a roar, a massive rack slashing through the low-lying branches of a tree directly behind him and turning the leaves to confetti.

"I repeat," I told Rustin as I carefully felt my toes inside my sneakers. I thought the damage was limited to the baby toe on my left foot, but the whole foot felt as if it had been broiled so I wasn't sure. "What is happening?"

The sky erupted behind the deer, the squirrels, and the very angry bunnies and a terrifying mass of small black critters flew out of the trees, dancing and weaving on the air as they headed right for us.

"Bats!" I screamed, ducking as the cloud of flying rodents shot beneath the gazebo and sailed over our heads. Claws caught in my hair and scratched my skin. My hands flew up as something bit the back of my neck. Random bolts of energy sizzled on the air as I swung my arms to get them away from me.

My magic pinged wildly around me in my panic, and one of Rustin's energy bolts seared past my nose, close enough to singe the hairs in my nostrils. I hit the ground, covering my head against Rustin's manic flares of magic.

The thundering sound of hooves told me the deer were coming. I could only assume the rest of them were coming too.

"Rustin!" I screamed, unable to get up off the floor as the bats swooped and chittered, attacking my skin, hair, and clothes. I felt as if I had a hundred bleeding bites over my arms, neck, and ankles.

Cooperire! Rustin screamed.

A soothing blanket of energy settled over me. The bats suddenly shot upward, slamming against the top of the magical barrier Rustin had created around us and sinking through, expelled by his magical command.

Shuddering, I shoved at my hair, feeling as if there were bats still crawling around in it, and pushed to my feet.

My eyes went wide. "Splintered toad toothpicks!"

6

HOLY BELLIGERENT BUNNIES!

*R*ed-eyed bunnies, slavering deer, growling raccoons, and angrily chattering squirrels flew toward us, a fog of hate shrouding their usually benign gazes. A silver haze of magic filtered through them, dusting them with dark energy and urging them forward, into battle.

Hovering above the salivating mishmash of nature's warriors was Maleficent's staff, the orb at its crux pulsing with angry light. The familiar high-pitched buzz filled the air, seeming to drive the animals crazy with rage.

I glanced at Rustin. He was staring in horror at the usually timid and basically harmless creatures leaping from the grass and hitting the edge of the platform, intent on doing us harm.

Above my head, bats pounded against the

barrier, tiny faces tight with animus and sharp teeth bared.

"This is horrifyingly weird," I told the ghost witch.

He slowly dragged his gaze away from the attackers, which were systematically flinging themselves at his barrier, creating ripples in its surface that made panic flare in my chest. "You need to neutralize the staff," he told me. "Once you have it under your control, the spell the artifact put on the animals will be extinguished."

Oh, yeah. Just neutralize the staff. Why hadn't I thought of that? I didn't want to ask, aware of how stupid it made me look since I was basically asking Rustin how to do my job, but the words jammed themselves into my mouth and wrenched my teeth open to jump out. "How do I do that?"

Rustin's gaze narrowed. "You're the KoA. You figure it out."

Yeah, thanks for that. Maybe I didn't feel bad the witch was stuck in a frog.

Meanwhile, back at the bubble, we were surrounded by angry, hate-filled forest critters, all flinging themselves against the barrier in an effort to get to us.

Hovering above the chaos, the staff seemed perfectly content to watch its makeshift army degrade Rustin's magic bubble. It hadn't moved since arriving at the gazebo.

I flung out my hand and sent a thick ribbon of keeper magic toward the artifact. The magic shot away from me and slammed into the staff, hard enough to knock it backward a few feet. Unfortunately, the defiant artifact didn't answer the summons. Instead, its orb sent out a fresh jolt of dark energy to increase the resistance around us.

Millions of crickets were suddenly slamming against the bubble, creating tiny pocks in its clear surface with every attack. The bugs were succeeding where the larger animals hadn't. Or maybe Rustin's energy was degrading under the combined attack of so many magic-enraged critters.

"Use the book!" Rustin shouted as a large crack started at the bottom of the bubble, and the first crickets made their way inside. I jumped as the bugs flung themselves at my legs and frantically kicked out at them, not wanting to slaughter them for something they couldn't control, but unwilling to have them crawling all over me either.

The crack widened. Something much more dire slipped through, its red eyes peering at me with blatant rage.

I couldn't help it. I screamed like a girl. The spider was half the size of my palm, with hairy legs and a fat, striped body.

"I hate spiders!" I screamed to Rustin. As it scurried forward, I screamed again and hit the back of the bubble, kicking at the nasty thing as three more spiders entered the crack I'd inadvertently widened when I'd fallen.

A chipmunk squeezed through after the spiders, its tiny teeth bared and claws flashing.

In a fit of desperation, I threw keeper magic toward the chipmunk.

The poor thing squeaked and released its bladder, its fur standing straight up on its tiny body.

Something flashed past and slashed at the spiders, sending them toward the barrier, where they sank through and disappeared.

Wicked wound around my legs.

"Where have you been, buddy?"

"Meow!" He leaped off the ground, and I barely caught him in my surprise. As soon as his body curled into my arms, I felt a surge of energy that nearly lifted me off the floor of the gazebo. It burned through me in an almost painful wave, making every hair on my body stand at attention and my breath huff out as if someone had punched me in the gut.

Wicked nipped gently at my arm. His tail smacked against my side. I got the message. Loud and clear. Lifting my hand, I flung another ribbon of keeper magic toward the staff.

The energy exploded away from my fingers with an ear-popping whoosh of magic that disintegrated Rustin's bubble and sent the forest friends flying back toward the trees. A thick gray fog filled the gazebo, odorless and dense enough to obscure everything beyond the perimeter of the structure.

The world went silent, except for the soughing of something flying through the mist. Wicked jumped from my arms just as the staff shot through the fog and I flung up my hand to catch it. The green orb flashed once more and then went dark.

The artifact was subdued.

The mist slowly oozed away. When I sent my gaze around the grassy boundary, I saw that the animals had also dispersed.

All that was left was one cute, fluffy bunny nibbling on the grass under the silvery moonlight. Seeing me watching it, the bunny lifted its head from the grass, wiggled its fluffy tail, and hopped away into the trees.

I sagged downward, my grip unrelenting on the staff. Reaching into my pocket, I pulled out the miniaturized Book of Pages and it exploded into full size at my touch. Balancing it on my knee so I could keep hold of the staff, I touched the cover and, as it warmed and rolled, I thought of the toxic magic room at Croakies. The familiar room oozed upward from the page. I slapped the orb end of the staff against it, watching as the orb began to spin and twist and then soaked into the page like water on a soft cloth.

I slammed the book closed and sagged to my knees on the floor.

Wicked wound around me, purring loudly. I rested my hand on his back, scratching in front of his tail. "Thanks for the boost, little buddy."

His response was a wide yawn. He took off toward the car and stood up on his back legs, batting at the door with his paw and meowing at me.

"Yeah, I'm tired too," I told him. It had been a long day. And, I realized with a jolt of weariness that dragged my shoulders offline. It wasn't over. I still had a mess to clean up at Croakies.

I was so busy feeling sorry for myself that I didn't even notice Rustin was gone until I opened the car door and watched Wicked curl up in the seat Rustin had been floating above on the ride over.

I'd walked all over the gazebo lawn looking for the ghost witch, calling out as I searched, but didn't find him. I finally decided he must have been blown back to where he'd come from like most of the animals had been under the wave of energy my cat and I had created. In Rustin's case, that would be Croakies, so Wicked and I headed home.

All the lights were on as I pulled up in front of my bookstore. I tried to remember if I'd left them on and decided I hadn't. Worry spiked.

I hurried toward the door and found it unlocked.

Shoving it open and rushing inside, I looked into the startled face of my assistant. "Oh." Sebille was holding Cinderella's wand and wearing a white apron. A streak of dirt slashed across her cheek, and she looked just like a red-haired, pointy-eared Cinderella. All she was missing was a song on her lips.

Goddess help me, don't let Sebille sing. She had a voice like a vulture with strep throat and a clogged nose.

Sebille straightened from the pile of glass she was turning back into the front window. As I watched, golden stars slipped from the wand and surrounded the shattered glass, lifting it into the air and assembling it into a shape that exactly matched the hole in the window. The reassembled glass slid into place with a soft pop.

I looked around the room, a grin finding my face. "It's all back to normal."

Sebille blew on the tip of the wand, spinning it in her fingers, and sticking it into one of the big pockets on the front of the frilly white apron. "This thing rocks. I'm using it on my place next."

I narrowed my gaze on her. "Your place?"

She seemed to miss the sarcasm in my question, simply nodding enthusiastically. "Did you get the staff?"

"I did. You should have seen it, Sebille, it was really cool..." My cell phone rang, cutting off my story about the gazebo, Wicked, and my greatly enhanced magic.

"Grym," I told her, looking at the name on the screen. "Hey, Detective. How's the investigation going?"

"Good," he said, his voice breaking on the word.

I frowned. "Are you okay? You sound different."

He cleared his throat. "I think I might be coming down with something."

"Don't give it to me, whatever it is. I don't need to be sick right now."

He coughed. "Yeah, me neither. I was calling to tell you that I think I've found the boyfriend who sells cosmetics. Are you interested in coming with me to talk to him tomorrow?"

I frowned, wondering at the detective's sudden interest in having me involved in every facet of the case. But I realized, as he probably had, that we might as well work it together, rather than investigating along parallel lines. "Sure. What time?"

"Ten..." he cleared his throat when his voice squeaked and tried again. "Ten AM. I'll pick you up at Croakies."

"Okay. See you in the morning." I hung up and stared at my phone.

"Is there something wrong?" Sebille asked.

I shook my head. "No. He just sounds different. I think he's getting sick and he wants me to come with him to talk to a witness tomorrow."

Sebille nodded. "Eat some of that fruit Lea brought you. You need lots of Vitamin C. I'll make you a special citrus tea in the morning."

I narrowed my gaze on her. "Who are you, and why are you being nice to me?"

Sebille snorted. "I think this wand might have done something to me. I was singing at Mr. Slimy, dancing around his tank earlier." She shook her head. "I've been whistling too."

I grimaced. "How'd the frog take the singing?"

She shrugged. "I think he was trying to drown himself in his pond, but it wasn't deep enough."

I laughed. "I don't blame him. You couldn't carry a tune in a suitcase with piano key lining."

"Har!" she said, sneering.

There's the Sebille I knew and loved. "Speaking about Mr. Slimy, you haven't seen Rustin have you?"

"I haven't been looking for him. Why?"

I explained to her what had happened at the gazebo.

"Lizard nipples!" she exclaimed. "You blew everything out of the gazebo?"

"Yeah," I said, frowning again. "I hope I didn't hurt Rustin."

"You don't have that kind of oomph," she told me thoughtfully. "How did that happen?"

"Rustin said the gazebo enhances magical energy. That, plus Mr. Wicked adding his enhancing powers to the mix, must have added up to a whale-bladder-sized magical whammy."

"Sweet Caroline!" she said, punching me on the arm. "Look at you, magicking like the grown-ups."

I made a face at her. "I'm exhausted. I need to go to bed. It sounds like tomorrow's going to be another wild one."

She nodded. "I'll see you in the morning."

I almost said, "You'll see me when you come upstairs," but decided in my great weariness it might come out sounding resentful so I bit my tongue. Instead, I walked over and looked down at Mr. Slimy. He was still sitting in his pond, probably in case Sebille decided to serenade him again, and his bulgy black gaze was locked on me. "Hey buddy, is your passenger onboard?"

Slimy blinked at me, his throat working as he gave me blank face. "No?" I sighed. "Okay." I started to turn away.

I'm hungry.

I turned to Sebille. "You can have some of my apple if you want. There's still a lot left."

She was gone. The connecting door between the bookstore and the artifact library was open.

You promised to bring me bugs.

I yelped and jumped backward, Slimy's blank gaze following my movement.

No. It wasn't possible. Then I had a thought. Moving closer, I asked, "Rustin?"

The frog just stared back at me. "Come on, Rustin. This isn't funny."

Nothing.

I shook my head. "I'll grab you some crickets." After relying on live bugs we caught in and around the store for several days, Sebille and I finally searched online to discover what frogs liked to eat. We discovered we could buy live crickets and mealworms for Mr. Slimy's gastronomic pleasure. Worms too, but there was no way I was handling a worm. Ugh!

A few minutes later, I turned off the lights and made sure all the locks were engaged, both physical and magical, and climbed the stairs to my apartment.

The door was, as usual, open a crack. I carefully shoved it wider so it didn't smack into Sebille's furniture and rubbed my tired eyes as I stepped into the apartment. I started to yawn, but jerked to a stop, my yawn cut short by a shock of surprise.

"What is happening?" I asked again, thinking I should just tattoo the question on my forehead.

All of Sebille's furniture was gone.

My rooms were back to normal. Except, they felt strangely, unnaturally quiet.

Great galloping gargoyles! Where was Sebille?

7

YOUTH IS NOT FOR THE FAINT OF HEART

J'd looked all over both sides of Croakies but hadn't found Sebille. She also hadn't answered her phone, so I'd tried calling Lea to see if she was in the greenhouse with the other Fae. Lea had assured me she'd seen my assistant within the last hour and she'd been fine.

Finally, since her furniture was gone, I decided Sebille must have found another apartment and forgotten to tell me. I would have jumped up and down with happiness, but I was too tired to get my toes off the ground.

Eight hours later, I was still too tired to get my toes off the ground. I'd had nightmares all night long about being old and wrinkled and being attacked by a shrinking gun.

Don't laugh, haven't you ever seen Men in Black?

Yeah, like all good humor being based in truth, all good movies are too.

In fact, I'd heard a shrinking artifact actually existed. Though I'd never clapped eyes on it.

Shoving a tangled ribbon of long brown hair out of my eyes, I yawned widely.

I stared at my tea, thinking that I might need to resort to coffee for an extra jolt of caffeine.

My phone rang and I looked at the name on the screen.

Grym again.

I sighed. The man was quickly moving from the persistent column into the annoying one. "Hello, Detective," I said, following up the greeting with a jaw-wrenching yawn. "What's up?"

"Naida..." His voice broke on my name, coming through the line with a higher pitch than it should have. "I'm sorry to bother you so early."

I frowned, pulling the phone away from my ear and looking at the name again. The detective didn't sound like himself. "Do you have a cold or something? Your voice sounds funny."

"No. I've just got a frog in my throat."

And I'd thought it was bad to have a frog in a fish tank. "Try drinking some lemon and ginger tea," I advised.

"I'll do that. I'm calling because it seems we have another artifact situation."

I came instantly alert. "Another..." I wasn't sure what to call it. "fetus" didn't feel right. "Embryo?"

"I'm afraid so. Can I pick you up in a few minutes? I'd like you to search the apartment for the artifact."

I glanced at the clock on my wall. Shaped like a frog that looked a lot like Mr. Slimy, it usually made me smile. At the moment, it just made me want to yawn again. "I have to open Croakies in half an hour."

"Can you open a little late?"

I could. But if things turned out anything like they had the day before, it would be more than a *little* late.

My door rattled under a thunderous knocking I recognized all too well. Sebille opened it a minute later, peering inside. "Do you want me to run to the bakery?"

I shook my head. "I need to go out for a bit. Can you hold down the fort?"

Sebille sighed, looking disappointed that she wouldn't get her daily dose of sugar and fat. "I'll bring donuts back," I said, sweetening the pot.

Her dejected expression brightened. "Okay." She slammed the door before I could ask where she'd gone the previous night.

"Keeper?" a high-pitched voice said into my ear, followed by a firm throat clearing.

I grimaced. "You should probably see a doctor about that, Detective."

Grym chose not to respond to my good advice. "I'll pick you up in ten minutes."

He disconnected before I could argue that I needed more time. "*Dormouse dandruff!*" I exclaimed, jabbing the button to end the call. "It will take me that long just to brush my hair."

I rolled into the bookstore twenty minutes later to find a clearly annoyed Detective Grym standing by the front door, scratching one arm and glaring at me.

I'd finally given up trying to wrangle my tangled mass of hair into any kind of tidiness and decided to pull it into a messy ponytail instead. To compensate for that breach of good grooming, I'd spent extra time on eyeliner and mascara in a smoky charcoal gray color that I hoped would emphasize the blue of my eyes.

I'd pulled on my best pair of yoga pants and a tee-shirt that exclaimed, "Pink Elephants are my Crack" and a pair of black sneakers that I hoped would look like dress shoes.

I was too tired to dress in clothes that constricted.

It was a thing. When I was tired or stressed, I tended to want to burrow into soft fleece and eat cookies. The yoga pants and tee were my compromise on that desire.

Grym's gaze focused on the dancing pink elephant on my shirt and he rolled his eyes. "Are you finally ready?"

I blinked, looking carefully at the growly detective. It wasn't just his voice that had changed. "Are you wearing makeup?" I asked him.

He frowned, running a hand through his dark hair and sending it into spikes. "Of course not. Why would you ask me that?"

"Because your face is as smooth as a baby's bottom." I got closer, peering at him until he growled low in his throat. He didn't look anything like the grizzled gargoyle detective I sort of knew and kind of liked. "And you have no laugh lines."

He turned away and grabbed the door. "Let's go. We're late."

As we left, Sebille called out, "Two frosted chocolate cake with sprinkles!"

Giving her a thumbs up, I hurried after Grym. I narrowed my gaze on him as he reached down and hiked up his jeans, realizing that he looked leaner than before. "Have you lost weight too?"

"No, I haven't lost weight, Naida Keeper," he all but growled out.

I lifted a hand in surrender. "Okay, sorry."

We were silent for the first few minutes, him glaring straight ahead and me trying to decide if making conversation was worth the risk of having my head bitten off. I finally decided silence was golden. I'd wrangled a Black Widow spider the size of my fist once. She'd tried to bite off my head with jaws that extended on several hinges and had almost succeeded.

I wasn't in a hurry to repeat that experience.

But when I saw him turn into the *Enchanted Glenn Apartments*, I spoke up. "What are we doing here again?"

Grym parked in front of the manager's building. "The victim is the apartment manager."

I blinked in surprise, remembering the sour-tempered woman with the long, melting wax face. "Seriously? She didn't strike me as the type to use expensive cosmetics."

"No," Grym said, the scowl replaced by a thoughtful look. "She didn't."

The room looked exactly the same as it had when we'd been there before. With the exception of the missing manager.

Or should I say, the greatly reduced manager?

We found the telltale speck on the seat of her office chair, but the moisture the embryo was resting in had soaked down into the upholstery, creating a dark spot instead of a puddle.

I grimaced. "This is just grisly."

Grym seemed to agree. His full, well-shaped lips were contorted with disgust. We looked around for a container of cream or some kind of lotion but found nothing.

As before, my keeper magic didn't find anything I could call forward as an artifact. It did, however, circle around the manager's chair for a few beats as if confused before dissipating with a soft hiss.

I frowned. "Someone has to be bringing the stuff in and taking it back out with them when they leave."

Grym didn't look convinced. He stood behind the manager's chair, staring down at it and scratching a spot on the underside of his forearm. "It has to be here somewhere."

I shook my head. "Sorry, but it's not. If the artifact had been there, my seeking magic would have found it."

He slammed a fist down on the desktop, making me jerk in surprise.

"Detective?"

His hands clenched at his sides, his gaze sliding to me, filled with hostility. Almost as quickly as the emotion washed over him, it slid away. "I'm sorry, Naida." Scrubbing a hand over his face, he fixed me with a worried gaze. "I've been trying to deny it but, something's wrong with me..."

The last couple of words came out on a broken squeak. I walked over and grabbed his hand and looked at the spot he'd been scratching. It was red from the nearly constant scraping, but the skin was smoother than a baby's bottom.

A sudden, horrifying thought made my breath

hitch. My gaze shot to his, and I saw understanding there.

He'd already figured it out.

"How?" I asked, wanting to step away in case it was catching. I forced myself to stand still, holding onto his wrist. My touch was the only comfort I could give him.

"I must have rubbed against the spot on the tablecloth when I was examining the table," Grym finally said. He stared at his arm. "I've been trying to make excuses for the signs that I'm infected. But it's becoming nearly impossible to do."

He'd brushed against the greasy circle on the cloth, getting some of the artifact on his arm. It must have been just a tiny amount, which was why it was working so slowly on him. But slow or not, I doubted the artifact would stop its forward progress until it returned him to his earliest state.

My gaze slid back down to Ms. Wexille's chair. "We need to find this artifact fast." I hadn't meant to speak the thought out loud. I realized I had when Grym shifted away, tugging his arm from my grip. "Don't you think I realize that, Naida Keeper?"

I bit back a sigh. I hadn't meant to pile on.

Stupid, stupid me.

Grym disappeared into another room in the apartment for several moments. I could hear him searching furniture and opening doors. I did the same, exploring the kitchen and the living area for anything that looked like a greasy cosmetic cream.

I didn't find anything and apparently Grym didn't either.

When he came back to the front room a while later, he didn't even look my way. "Let's get out of here," Grym said, his long strides eating up the distance to the front door more quickly than seemed possible. I wondered if his youthful changes were internal as well, or if the outside youth would war with the time-worn organs and create a new type of damage that couldn't be seen.

Shaking my head, I hurried after him. I had no desire to join Grym in finding out. But I also knew I couldn't just let nature...or unnatural magic...take its course and remove a new friend from my life.

My heart pounding with fear, I stopped at the door. "I..." When Grym turned back to me, his jaw rigid and his eyes dark with fear, I gave him a tight smile. "I'm going to try searching one more time for the artifact. I'll meet you in the car in a few minutes."

He nodded, clearly happy to get out of the place. "Don't touch anything, Naida," he said softly.

I would have been annoyed if I hadn't recognized the worry in his gaze. He hadn't been warning me about disturbing a crime scene. He'd been telling me not to risk contaminating myself.

As he'd done.

Five minutes later, I shoved a small, plastic container inside my pocket and headed for Grym's charcoal-gray car. As a gargoyle, the car suited him perfectly. If gargoyles became cars, they would turn into Grym's boxy SUV.

He eyed me as I slid into my seat. "Ready?" I asked, to spur him on. "I need to stop at Enchanted Bakery before you take me back."

He put the car into gear. "I heard. Two frosted chocolate cake donuts with sprinkles." He smiled at the last part. "How old is your assistant, anyway?"

I shook my head. "Sprites never outgrow their love of sugar. Sugar is comfort. Especially when it's wrapped around fat and chocolate."

He snickered softly, looking more relaxed than he'd appeared earlier. It had apparently been good for him to share his worries.

"I...um..."

He glanced my way. "Spit it out, Keeper."

"I'm going to consult with Madeline Quilleran about your...issue." I fully expected him to argue with me. He didn't, simply nodding after thinking about it for a moment.

That, more than anything, told me how worried he was.

Twenty minutes later, I stepped out of the boxy SUV and looked at him. "I'll let you know what Madeline tells me."

"Thanks."

I started to close the door.

"Wait!"

I glanced back his way.

He pointed to the small, white paper sack sitting on my seat. "You forgot a bag."

"I didn't forget that," I told him. I winked. "I thought you could use a few sprinkles in your life."

I closed the door before he could shove the bag toward me, but I turned back before opening the door to Croakies.

As Grym pulled out into traffic, he took a large bite of the donut I'd left for him. I grinned.

Sebille nearly tackled me at the door, grabbing the bag. "I'm starving."

I tried to grab it back. "Two of those are mine," I told her.

"Whatever," she stuck a hand into the greasy sack and pulled out her first donut.

"I got you three," I told her by way of sucking up.

Her eyes narrowed as she chewed. She swallowed. "Why? What are you up to?"

"I might need your help with something," I said, grimacing.

Her gaze still narrowed, Sebille shoved the donut into her mouth on another bite. "Bwhat?" Crumbs flew as I grabbed the bag and extracted my first cream-filled donut.

"Can you manage things alone here for a while? I need to go talk to Lea about an artifact."

Thankfully, Sebille swallowed before speaking again. "Why can't she come here?"

"She could..." I dithered, trying to decide how much to tell my nosy assistant.

"You're not going to Lea's, are you?"

I grimaced. "I am. But then I'm going someplace else."

Sebille lowered the donut, her gaze filled with suspicion. "Where else?"

"CoughQuilleransCough."

"Did you just say the Quilleran's?"

I started to stuff the donut into my face to keep from answering, but Sebille reached out and snagged my wrist. "Why are you going to Madeline Quilleran's again? You barely escaped with your life the last time."

Okay, that was a bit of an exaggeration. Madeline hadn't tried to hurt me. But her show of force when I'd shown up uninvited had made it clear she easily could.

And, she'd told me that was my one pass. The implication was clear. If I showed up uninvited again, she was going to make sure I understood why that was a bad idea.

"Don't be such a drama queen," I told Sebille.

I almost smiled at that. Usually, that was her accusation to me.

8

THE PLOT THICKENS - UNEVENLY

I ran into Mrs. Foxladle on my way to Lea's. I'd only pressured a temporary backup from Sebille. She was holding out on promising me the whole day until I got Lea's input on the contents of the plastic container.

I was frustrated by the lost time in explaining everything to Sebille and in a hurry. It took me a beat to realize who I'd nearly bowled over and adjust my attitude appropriately. Looking into the elderly woman's pale, careworn face, I gave in to an impulse to hug her. "How are you feeling, Mrs. Foxladle?"

"I've been better, hon. Could we speak to you for a moment?"

I frowned. "We?"

Footsteps on the sidewalk brought my head around. The early morning sunshine glinted off the graying head of Franny Clauss and highlighted a network of fine wrinkles I hadn't noticed before. "Hello, Naida," Franny said, smiling sadly. "We're sorry to bother you again."

I shook my head. "No. Not at all. Come inside. We'll have tea."

Sebille looked up from the book she was reading behind the counter as I came back inside. She slid a questioning gaze over the two older ladies, frowning.

"Sebille," I said, in a warning tone, "will you please make tea for Mrs. Foxladle and Ms. Clauss?"

Though Sebille gave me a look that told me she'd like to snip my fingernails off down to my knuckles, she came around the counter and headed for the tea station.

I pointed to the small, round table near the bookshelves. "Please, have a seat ladies. And tell me what I can do to help."

Behind me, I could almost hear Sebille's pointy ears perk up. The slamming around of tea making items softened a bit, no doubt so she could eavesdrop better.

I sat down with the two women and crossed my legs, waiting.

After sharing a look with Franny, Mrs. Foxladle spoke first. "I wasn't entirely honest with you about why I missed book club this week," she told me, her papery cheeks pinkening with embarrassment. "It wasn't because of the book we selected..."

"Well, it was true that you hate that book,"

Franny added helpfully. "Heaven knows, you've made no secret of it."

Mrs. Foxladle flipped her fingers toward her friend. "It's not my favorite of Dane Andress's work. She's so competent with a smoothly flowing sentence. Her descriptions are to die for, putting me right inside the story from the first page. But that book was just too uneven in tone for me. I couldn't feel the tension between the characters and the world-building was less than satisfactory."

"True, but the plot tension more than makes up for it," Franny offered, settling back in her chair as she warmed to her subject. "The secondary characters are four-dimensional." She giggled like a schoolgirl. "I just want to bring that pot-bellied pig home and dress her in pink ruffles."

Mrs. Foxladle rolled her eyes, and I hid a smile behind my hand. "You're much too easily led into the net, Franny. A cute pig is not enough to overcome the flaws in the story. I can't believe you bought the whole missing heir subplot. It was just too outrageous to believe."

"I couldn't disagree more," Franny began, leaning forward with an earnest look on her face to jump into the argument with both feet.

I cleared my throat as Sebille settled two dainty cups of tea in front of the ladies.

They blinked in my direction as if they'd

forgotten I was there. "Oh my," Mrs. Foxladle said, chuckling softly. "I do apologize, hon. When Franny and I get started arguing a book, we sometimes forget the world beyond our opinions even exists."

Franny nodded, sipping her tea. She closed her eyes and sighed when she tasted it, giving Sebille a bright smile. "This is delicious, dear. Thank you so much."

"Sebille is tea-talented," I told the ladies, throwing my assistant a smile in thanks. "Now, what is it you wanted to tell me." I grinned, "Other than to not buy any more copies of 'Heiring on the Side of Murder.'"

Mrs. Foxladle's eyes went wide. "You recognized the book we were referring to? Good for you, Naida."

I gave her a non-committal smile. I'd actually seen the books lying on the table at the crime scene, but I didn't want to distract them again by going into that. I'd never read the book myself, not being a fan of Dane Andress's work. I agreed with Mrs. Foxladle. It was a bit uneven for my taste.

"As I was saying," Mrs. Foxladle continued. "I didn't miss the meeting because of the book. I stayed away because I had a terrible quarrel with Celia."

Oh, oh. "What did you fight about?" I asked, hoping it wasn't something that could be seen as a motive for murder.

Mrs. Foxladle skimmed Franny a look. The other

woman nodded in what I perceived to be encouragement. She sighed. "I'm afraid Celia was misusing the meetings."

I relaxed slightly. That sounded pedestrian enough so as not to inspire Grym to handcuff the sweet elderly woman. "In what way?"

"She'd begun selling those horrible cosmetics to us, sometimes taking up so much time during the meeting we didn't have time to talk about the books." Mrs. Foxladle's small face puckered with disgust. "As a founding member of the Enchanted Reading Club, I was very vocal about my displeasure. I even went so far as to demand she stop peddling her junky products at the meetings." She glanced at Franny again, earning herself a pat on the hand. "I'm convinced she selected that book hoping I wouldn't show up for the meeting this week."

Franny looked for a moment like she would disagree and then pinched her lips closed.

"Did she try to sell these items every week?" I asked.

"Yes," Franny said, nodding. "But it wasn't too bad at first. She'd simply place a bunch of samples out on the sideboard, and we'd take some if we wanted, asking questions about the products as warranted. But lately..." Franny's lips pursed. "She'd been giving us the hard sell. Glenny and I weren't the only ones who disapproved."

Glenny must be a nickname for Glenis, Mrs. Foxladle's first name. "Were you vocal about your disapproval too?" I asked Franny.

"Of course." She slid a sheepish look toward Mrs. Foxladle. "Not as strongly as Glenny of course, but enough that Celia and I had a few arguments. In fact, that's why I really got to the meeting late, last night," she admitted, her face flushing. "I'd gone early to talk to her about it. I'm afraid we fought about her doing the hard sell behind Glenny's back."

I nodded. "How did Celia react to your anger?"

Franny's fingers knitted together, a clear sign of her nervousness. "She was horrible to me. I ended up storming out, not intending to return. But I'd forgotten my phone and I didn't want to leave it there. The way Celia had been acting lately, I was afraid she might stomp on it or something."

Sebille set a cup of tea in front of me. "Would you ladies like another cup?"

Both eagerly accepted. I knew Sebille was hanging close so she could listen in, but I was okay with that. I wanted to get her opinion about what I was learning after the ladies left.

"Celia's behavior was not normal for her?"

"Not until recently," Mrs. Foxladle said. "She'd been getting steadily worse since she took on the sales position."

"Worse how?" I asked.

"Pushy," Mrs. Foxladle said.

"Insulting," Franny added. "She'd taken to pointing all our flaws out to us so she could sell us some magical cream to fix whatever it was." Franny shook her head. "It had gotten so bad I overheard a couple of the others talking about leaving the book club."

Mrs. Foxladle's gaze darkened. "That breaks my heart, Fran. I didn't realize the others felt that way."

Franny nodded. "You can imagine..."

Mrs. Foxladle nodded, apparently filling in the gap in what Franny hadn't said and agreeing with it. "The woman was a menace."

"Was there anyone else?" I asked, hesitating as Sebille gave them fresh cups of tea. "Anyone outside of the club, who might have wanted to harm Celia?" I finished a beat later.

"Everyone, I presume," Franny said matter-of-factly. "She was a shrew to everyone."

Well, that just isn't helpful, I thought. I decided to go in another direction. "Can you give me any idea where the cosmetics came from that she was selling? I understand there was a young man who came to her home regularly. Did she get them from him?"

"I assumed it was some type of pyramid scam," Mrs. Foxladle said, settling her cup into the saucer. "She was so frantic to sell and she kept trying to get us to buy into selling them ourselves."

"Yes," Franny said, "I agree. I'm not sure it was

even about the cosmetics. I think it was just one of those companies that roped people into buying tons of the stuff and getting others to buy tons of the stuff and so on and so on."

I felt my eyes go wide. "Did Celia have a lot of the cosmetics somewhere? The police searched her home and didn't find any, except for what was on her counter in the bathroom."

Franny and Mrs. Foxladle shared shocked looks.

"Yes, oh my, she had boxes and boxes of the stuff in her spare bedroom," Mrs. Foxladle said. "I can't believe they didn't find it."

I couldn't either. I'd have to talk to Grym about that spare room. If the boxes weren't there when the police searched the apartment. I had to wonder where they'd gone.

I all but shoved the two older ladies out the door moments later, promising to keep them updated on the investigation. I wasn't entirely comfortable with the new glint in Mrs. Foxladle's eyes. It appeared she might be embracing the mystery lover in her soul as a means of dealing with her friends' deaths.

The last thing I needed was for the two ladies to get hurt...or worse...sticking their well-honed mystery snouts into the current mess. They had no idea what type of artifact they might be up against.

At least one of them had *no* idea, I corrected myself. Franny Clauss might well understand what had happened to their friends. I only hoped she knew enough to keep Mrs. Foxladle from getting too close to the investigation.

Sebille came back into the store with the freshly washed tea things, sliding a look toward me as I pulled my purse out from under the counter. "I hope you've changed your mind about going to Madeline Quilleran's home."

I started to respond but was rudely interrupted by a snotty voice. "Have you lost your tiny little mind, sorceress?"

I swung around as Rustin floated into the room. He crossed his arms over his chest and glared down his long nose at me. "If you have a death wish, there are much easier ways to die."

I rolled my eyes, turning to Sebille to share my derision of the ghost witch. Unfortunately, she'd focused an equally judgy glare on me. Even Mr. Slimy, currently pressed up against the glass on the near end of his glass home, seemed to be giving me a froggy glare.

I gave an uncomfortable laugh. "I'll be fine. Madeline and I have an understanding."

Rustin snorted out a laugh.

"And what is that? You understand that you're a

bug on the rug and she understands that she can smash you to smithereens underneath her shoe?" Sebille asked.

I shook my head. "I've got this. Stop worrying, you two."

Sebille's response was to cross her arms over her flat chest like Rustin and deepen her glower. "You're taking unnecessary risks."

"What would you have me do, Sebille?" I asked. "Five women are dead because of this artifact. This is bad."

"Ribbit."

I glared back at Mr. Slimy. "Your input is not required, frog."

Oh sure, disrespect the frog. Why not? What's he going to do about it?

My gaze slid to Rustin and narrowed. "And, what exactly do you believe makes the frog worthy of my respect?"

Rustin blinked in surprise, frowning. "I didn't..."

"Meow." Wicked's soft form wound itself around my ankles, his tail trailing over my shins as he gave me soft eyes. At least my cat didn't seem to be judging me. I scooped him up, burying my face in his fragrant fur. "Hey, buddy."

He whacked me on the nose with a tiny bit of claw.

"Ouch!"

Okay, maybe there was a tiny bit of judgment

there, after all. I gave a frustrated huff. "My job is to find and deal with artifacts. How am I supposed to do that without taking the occasional risk?"

"You take the occasional risk," Rustin said, seeming to agree with me. "But only when you have no other choice. It's not necessary to take this risk. Use what you have available to you, Keeper."

I stared at him a moment and then widened my gaze, shaking my head. "And that is...?"

"Me," he said. "Madeline is family. Let me contact her and set up a meeting."

I thought about it for a moment and then nodded. "That makes sense."

"I'm going with you," Sebille said, her glare telling me she wasn't bending.

I stuck my chin out, prepared to do battle. She lowered her dense red brows, looking like a freckle-faced, pointy-eared Brahma bull. I half expected her to paw the ground and snort.

Throwing my hands into the air, I gave in. "All right! You can come, Sebille. I guess I'll just have to close early."

"I'm coming too," Rustin said.

I didn't even attempt that battle. "All right."

I headed toward the door. "I'm going to talk to Lea." I turned back to Rustin at the door. "Tell Madeline Lea's coming too."

His brows climbed his forehead. "What? No,

Naida. Maddie's not going to want another witch in her home..."

"Too bad," I said. "I need Lea there to tell me if Madeline's being honest." When he shook his head, I wrenched the door open. "She's coming, Rustin. Whether you tell your aunt or not. There might be less blow-back if Madeline knows, but I'll leave that up to you."

9

FROG PEE HAPPENS

I found Lea in the greenhouse, harvesting herbs for her shop. She glanced up when I came through the door, a wide smile splitting her pretty round face. "Hey, Naida." She pushed to her feet, wiping her hands on the apron she'd tied on over her long, gauzy skirt and spotless white tee shirt. "I'm glad you came. I have more fruit for you."

Lea's fairy-touched garden was full to bursting with thriving plants, including a small orchard of apple, peach, and pear trees that Sindra, the Fae Queen, had planted to thank her for giving them a home in her greenhouse when their village in the Enchanted Forest had been razed by the Quillerans.

I glanced around at the oversized plants filling every box. The air was sweet with a mixture of lavender, mint, and roses. Each garden box was bulging with plants in different shades of green. "Wow, every time I come in here the gardens look bigger and healthier."

Lea beamed at me. "The fairies have been so generous. I'm truly blessed."

The sound of wings beating the air had my head snapping up. Three dragonfly-sized fae buzzed in my direction, Queen Sindra leading the arrow-shaped delegation. She was flanked by two of her advisors, but no soldiers.

I was touched that she trusted me enough not to bring guards.

I smiled, waving as she hurried toward me. "Naida, Keeper." She dipped her wings as she hovered before me, her tiny face aglow. "How are you this beautiful day?"

As always, I was struck by the sunniness of her personality, in direct contrast to her daughter's. Sebille was the cloud cover to her mother's golden sunlight.

"I'm fine, Queen Sindra. Your garden is lush." It was the strongest compliment I could give the fairy queen, made stronger by the fact that it was the truth.

She dipped her head in acceptance of the accolade, flushing with pleasure. "You're chasing an artifact."

"I am. A toxic one."

She cocked her head. "Sebille told me. Something about youth cream that takes people all the way back to their womb-state."

"Unfortunately, yes. Have you heard about such a thing before?"

She frowned. "Not specifically, no. But you might want to talk to the goblins."

I lifted my brows in surprise. "Goblins? I didn't know there were goblins in Enchanted."

"Oh, yes. They've lived here for centuries. Though they keep a very low profile as you can imagine."

I certainly could imagine. History and mythology had not been kind to the race. They'd gotten a bad rep in a lot of ways. Some of what they'd been accused of was real. They were exceedingly ugly creatures, prone to mischief and sometimes even treachery. But many of them were kind, and they could be very loyal to those they trusted.

Trust was both the key and the problem. Goblins didn't trust easily.

"Why do you think I should speak to the goblins?" I asked the queen.

"They have a cosmetics factory just outside Enchanted. Really mostly lotions and creams. I believe they have an anti-aging line. Maybe they know who could be responsible."

I nodded. "That's very helpful. Thank you."

She inclined her head and turned away, buzzing off without another word.

I looked at Lea. She was snuggling her little cat,

Hex, who looked a lot like Wicked except that her eyes were more golden where his tended toward orange and she was more delicate in build. Like a girl. "That was helpful."

Lea nodded. "I've been hearing rumors lately that the goblins are ramping up sales. I guess they have a competitor. I'm betting that competitor might be the one with the artifact."

I frowned. "They're not going to get very far if they keep killing off all their customers."

She grimaced. "There is that. It's a strange mess, isn't it?"

"Yeah." I glanced around. "Hey, do you think you could come with me to the Quilleran's today."

Her pretty turquoise eyes went round. "Madeline Quilleran's house? Are you crazy?"

"I don't think I am." I grinned. "Rustin's getting us an invite so we won't be going under threat of death this time."

She mock-shuddered, settling Hex back to the ground and watching with a grin as the cat loped in the direction the fairies had gone. She caught me smiling at the kitten and gushed. "I'm so happy to have her, Naida. I don't think I ever thanked you for giving her to me."

We'd rescued Wicked's littermates from the Quilleran witches, the bad side of the family, and I'd been thrilled when my friend had asked if she could keep one of them. The others were living with my friends. LA was a human familiar cat shifter and Deg was her witch. LA had a cat sanctuary in nearby *Illusion City* and she'd made sure the kittens had good homes. The best part was they'd all stayed with LA and her friends so Wicked and I could see them. "Don't be silly. I'm thrilled you kept her so she and Wicked can be best friends." And they were. The two cats spent much of every day together, exploring either Croakies or Lea's herbal shop together.

She frowned. "Why are you going to Madeline's today?"

I hesitated a moment, having second thoughts about showing her what I'd taken from the apartment manager's home. It was disturbing and would probably rock Lea's world in a bad way. But Lea lifted her brows as if she'd read my thoughts and held out her hand. "Let's see it."

After another moment's hesitation, I sighed, reaching into my purse and pulling out the small storage container. I carefully opened it and showed her the contents. She narrowed her gaze, leaning closer for a moment before her eyes went wide and she jumped back. "Ew!"

I nodded, clapping the lid back onto the container. "Yeah. It's gruesome. But I thought maybe Madeline, since she dabbles in dark magic, might be able to tell me something about who killed that poor woman if she had this."

Lea grimaced. "And you want me along, why?"

"Because I don't trust her. I need you there to tell me if she tries blowing smoke up my skirt."

Lea thought about it for a moment and then nodded. "Okay. When are we leaving?"

"As soon as we get the go-ahead from Rustin."

After much deliberation, I'd decided to take Berbie the Loving Bug on our trip back to the Enchanted Forest, just in case the Quilleran castle decided to be difficult again. Madeline Quilleran was a Power That Be. A member of a select group of magical decision-makers that kept an eye on the magic rabble and made sure we didn't do anything to compromise the safety of the whole.

As a person of some influence in the magical Universe, Madeline received extra protections, which included having her exact location hidden from anyone who might discover her identity and try to find her.

The previous time I'd visited, Berbie's special navigational prowess had located Madeline for me, aided by a little magical waterboarding to ensure the nav guy's unwilling cooperation.

I felt a little bad for encouraging the strong-arm tactics, but the nav guy did have a snotty, English-Butler-ish attitude which, admittedly, softened my guilt quite a bit.

If I was being honest, my decision to take Berbie was also selfish, based on the fact that he wasn't going to be with me much longer. His new owner had been located and she was coming to pick him up soon. I wanted one last adventure with the fun little car before he left.

Fortunately for us, our second visit to the castle in the forest didn't involve fighting with the nav. Apparently greasing the skids with the witch's permission worked wonders to smooth out those "unwelcome visitor" vibes I'd set into motion the last time.

Who knew?

It was a good thing too because Madeline's home was located in an entirely different part of the five-thousand-acre forest than it had been before. We'd have never found it without the Universe's help.

Berbie joyfully traversed the steep, winding forest roads, taking curves as if he were a magical car with no fear of crashing into bits at the bottom of the deep ravine bordering both sides of the narrow road.

I, however, nurtured enough fear for both of us. And if the ashy gray complexions and whiter-than-white knuckles predominating inside the crazy little car were any indication, my friends shared my fear of death by fiery explosion at the bottom of a ravine.

Even the ghost witch hovering next to Lea in the back seat looked wispier than usual. By contrast, the squishy green frog bus sitting on Lea's lap seemed deliriously oblivious.

"Goddess save us all," Sebille murmured from the front passenger seat, her hand moving in what could only be interpreted as the sign of the cross over her flat chest.

I narrowed my gaze on her, happy to concentrate on making fun of her instead of my imminent flaming death. "Did you just make the sign of the cross?" I asked, raising my brows.

Berbie bounced over a particularly beefy root in the road and tooted happily as we went airborne. He landed to a lusty chorus of gasps and swears and hit the gas, shooting off even faster toward the pitfalls ahead.

"I'm covering all my bases," she hissed. "I'd pray to Satan himself if it would make this terror stop sooner," Sebille murmured, her knuckles whiter than Rustin's ghostly white button-down.

Wary fairy, life is scary, intoned a voice inside my head.

I grinned at Rustin and he frowned.

With a final happy toot of his horn, Berbie plunged into a tree-shrouded stretch that seemed to have been designed by a stunt-driver with suicidal tendencies.

The hairpin turns were no longer bounded by a plunging landscape, but the enormous redwoods covering nearly every inch of ground would certainly do their part to pound us to bits if Berbie made a single misstep.

Lea's hands found Mr. Slimy and apparently squeezed too hard in her panic. He puked out a hearty, "Ribbit!" and then hopped from her lap into mine, landing on my jeans-clad thigh and quivering there. He resembled a green poop emoji with judgy bulging eyes.

I grimaced. "Who invited you over."

Red Rover, Red Rover, the frog can come over, the voice in my head chanted.

I shook my head, throwing Rustin a glance. "You're in rare form today, my friend."

Rustin's brows peaked.

Berbie's horn gave a quick, alarmed chirp and he threw on the brakes as we came out of a particularly sharp turn and found ourselves mere yards from the front door of Madeline's huge, dark house.

We skidded to a stop, taking the last five yards in a sideways crawl that sent dirt and rocks into the air as if someone had dropped a small bomb beneath Berbie's tires.

As we skidded to a stop mere inches from the rock wall bordering the very short drive, the car was silent, except for a slight panting sound coming from Berbie's engine.

Then Berbie cut his engine and the air thickened with foreboding.

Lea peered out her window, which was closest to the house. "What are those?"

As before when I'd been there, the long, dark roofline of the castle-like home was obscured by the massive feathery forms of Madeline's turkey vulture-like sentinels, their hostile red gazes locked on the little white car as if considering whether to have it with hot sauce or a nice Bearnaise.

I hadn't noticed them stalking our progress along the road as I had the last time, but I'd been kind of busy contemplating what it was going to feel like to die in a fiery crash.

"Madeline's forward watch," I said softly, realizing I was afraid to speak in a normal tone of voice, for fear the things would break their silent guard and attack.

Sebille's hand fluttered upward as if considering painting the air in front of her with the sign of the cross again.

"Did you bring your prayer rug?" I asked teasingly. "You could maybe get a few rounds of *God is Most Great* in before we go inside."

Sebille scowled over at me. "Don't think I haven't considered it."

"Should we get out of the car and ring the bell?" Lea asked, her hands clenched like two rigid knots on her lap.

"The last time the vulture things did something right before Madeline opened the door."

As if on cue, the big birds shifted on their perch, their wings lifting and lowering like a feathery wave that ran the length of the roof and then started back the other way.

"I feel like somebody should yell, 'Play ball'" Lea murmured.

As the last wave died at the end of the roof, the front door began to open, disappearing into the darkness inside the castle and showing us the tall, slender form waiting in the shadows.

I clenched the handle of my door. "That's our cue," I told my friends.

I climbed out and closed my door, turning back to find them all still inside, their eyes wide and their faces the color of paper.

Rustin's wispy form floated through the roof and headed up the stairs, his legs moving as if he was walking but his feet not touching the concrete beneath them.

Madeline emerged from the shadowy interior, giving Rustin a fond smile. "Hello, nephew."

He stopped in front of her. "Aunt Maddie. How are you?"

I followed him toward the door, my feet definitely hitting the concrete. I was pretty sure they were sticking to the stairs because it felt as if I were carrying half of their weight up with me on the bottom of my shoes.

Behind me, car doors softly opened and closed.

I turned to find Lea staring at the witch waiting for us by the door and Sebille eyeing the vultures, a threatening glare on her freckled face.

I smiled to myself. Sebille might be small and silly-looking in her bright red braids, striped socks, and glossy red shoes, but she would not go down easily.

She'd give those vulture things a run for their money. And then some.

I stopped in front of the witch. "Hey, Madeline."

Her gaze slid down to my hands, which were wrapped around a fat amphibian. I blinked in surprise. I didn't even remember grabbing Mr. Slimy before I climbed out of the car.

"You brought the frog," Madeline said, her features settling into a contented smile. "Good. I've been wanting to run some tests on him."

I blinked, not liking the sound of that. Before I knew what I was doing, I'd cuddled him close to my chest, shielding him with my hands. "Tests?" My head started shaking. "I can't let you hurt him."

She gave me a look filled with disgust. "I wouldn't harm him, Naida. That frog is special."

I narrowed my gaze, focusing it on the black-eyed, bulgy-throated green blob in my hands. Slimy focused the black orbs on me, seeming to take my measure as I took his. "*This* frog? Maybe you have him confused with another fat critter whose entire vocabulary consists of the word, ribbit."

Very funny, Keeper. I have some choice words you might like.

I rolled my eyes at Rustin.

Madeline's attention slid from me to the two women climbing the steps behind me. She gave Sebille a regal nod. "Princess Sebille."

Sebille's expression was neutral. She didn't speak, merely inclining her chin like royalty.

Madeline's gaze slid to Lea and narrowed, observing her for a beat before giving my friend a condescending smile. "Hello, Mistress Witch."

"This is my friend, Lea," I said. "She's helping me figure out what kind of artifact we're looking for."

Madeline's slender black brows rose a titch, Her clear brow creasing. "I see." The two words were filled with the conceit evident in every line of the Quilleran witch's demeanor. It seemed to say, why would you need this first-level herbal practitioner when you have me?

The shadows behind the door boiled and spit out a smaller, lighter version of Madeline onto the porch. Maude Quilleran grinned when she saw me, launching herself in my direction. "Naida Keeper! How are you? How's Mr. Wicked?"

Laughing, I wrapped my arms around the teen as she flung herself at me, giving her a hug. "I'm fine. Wicked's adorable. He's so happy to have his sister nearby to play with."

Maude pulled back, her pretty face alight with

happiness. "I need to come for a visit. I want to see them both."

"Hex is getting big," Lea told the young witch. "And fat!"

They shared a giggle at that. When we'd rescued the litter from Jacob Quilleran's home, they'd been filthy and undernourished.

"I'm so glad," Maude said, taking Lea's hands. Then she spotted Mr. Slimy and squealed, making the frog jump in my hand and pee.

"*Caterpillar suspenders,*" I grumbled as the warm liquid ran between my fingers and barely missed my sneakers.

Maude made a "sorry" face. "I'll take him if you want. You can wash up inside."

I nodded, handing him over to her and watching in awe as she lifted him, touching her nose to his and speaking softly.

"Come," Madeline said. "I'll show you where you can wash your hands."

10

WHAAAAAAT?

We sat around in an uncomfortable silence as Madeline opened the plastic container and looked inside. The powerful witch held her hand over the contents, emitting a silver light that filled the container and made the sides bulge and roll as if melting.

I threw Lea a worried glance. She shook her head, telling me not to worry.

Though I chewed the inside of my lip, I forced myself to sit back in my chair, my muscles relaxing just a titch.

I wouldn't totally relax until we were back in Berbie and heading back to Croakies. Then I thought of the little car's manic exuberance on the twisty, precarious roads and I tensed right back up again.

"Have you tried to read this?" Madeline asked, her piercing, yellow gaze finding Lea.

"Yes. I couldn't identify the signature, but an herbal illumination found ancient remnants in the magic."

Madeline inclined her chin, her expression flashing approval before she squelched it. "Ancient. Yes. I'm guessing Archaic Greece. Possibly one of the gods."

I felt my eyes go wide. "We have an ancient Greek god living in Enchanted?"

"Not necessarily." Madeline wiggled her fingers over the container and it dropped away, leaving only the gruesome contents floating in the air before her face.

I grimaced, looking away.

"But definitely someone with that ancestry."

"Queen Sindra mentioned goblins," Rustin said. When his aunt glanced his way, he went on. "They have ancient ties to the gods. It's possible they got hold of an artifact that holds ancient fountain-of-youth magic."

She frowned slightly, tilting her head as she returned her gaze to the embryo twirling in the air. "Possibly. But this smacks of magic malpractice. If someone is using old magic, they don't know what they're doing."

"What do you mean?" I asked.

Her yellow gaze burned into me, filled with

disapproval. "Isn't that obvious? Unless someone's looking for a unique way to kill people, they fell well short of their mark. If they were attempting to give youth, they went overboard by a deadly measure."

I certainly couldn't argue with that.

"Unless they weren't *giving* at all."

All eyes slid to Sebille. She held Madeline's piercing gaze without flinching.

"Explain," Madeline said, then added, "Please?" when Sebille stiffened with affront.

"Maybe they were *stealing* youth, rather than trying to give it."

"But that makes no sense," Lea argued. "Wouldn't they have targeted young people then?"

Sebille shook her head. "Consider auras."

Lea's frown deepened.

Huffing her frustration that we didn't immediately grasp her meaning, Sebille barely kept from rolling her eyes. I admired her restraint. wondering why she never showed that restraint with me.

"You need to separate aura or life force from the physical shell. A body might wither over time, but an aura thickens. Aura represents life and the richness of existence. We think of older people as having less youth and more age. But the reality is that their auras have collected more life than the auras of young people have. A baby's aura is thin and weak. A ninety-year-old's aura is dense and strong. If I was looking to add more life, or youth, I'd look at taking from an older person rather than a young one."

When we all continued to stare at her, speechless, she threw up her hands. "It's a simple math problem. It would take a dozen young people to create the same amount of life energy as one old person."

"Brilliant," Madeline murmured. "You're right, Princess. I hadn't thought of it that way."

Lea became agitated. Her gaze shot to Madeline's. "If we're looking for life force..."

"We can easily test for that," Madeline said, nodding.

"A simple Graves and Blench stain..."

"Yes," Madeline agreed. "And we can diversify the sample looking for sulfuric properties."

Lea stood. "I assume you have a lab?"

Madeline flicked her fingers toward the container on the ground. It flew up to encompass the sample again, the lid snapping on a beat later. She grabbed the container, motioning to Lea to follow. "Rustin, you may come with Mistress Witch Lea. The rest of you stay here."

I watched them disappear through a door that had popped open in the paneling and turned to Sebille. "What just happened?"

My assistant rolled her eyes.

See what I mean?

"Thanks to me, they're much closer to finding out who's got the artifact."

"Humble much?" I muttered, earning myself a glare from the freckled aura expert with pointy ears.

"Don't be a jealous derf," Sebille said snottily. "I can't help it if I'm good at thinking outside the box."

I snorted. That was a gargantuan understatement. Sebille's picture was probably in Shirley's Witch-a-Pedia next to the phrase, "outside the box".

The sound of wings beat the air, coming down the hall. I braced myself as Madeline's arrogant familiar, Rasputin glided through the door and landed lightly on the back of the chair Madeline had vacated. He peered down his beak at me, his beady silver gaze filled with derision.

"Where have you been, Ras?" I asked, deliberately using Madeline's pet name for him just to annoy.

He was much too easy. His feathers immediately ruffled, and he danced from foot to foot as he rolled them flat again. "I was tending to business, Keeper. Besides I didn't want to witness your humiliation," he intoned snottily. "Are you comfy here in the playroom while the adults are busy saving the world in the other room?"

Sebille lifted her hand, sparkly green energy drifting from her fingertips. "I have an idea, raven. How about I press you into my scrapbook and preserve you as a dry husk of a distant, unpleasant memory?"

He sniffed. "I'd like to see you try, bug."

Sebille shot to her feet, energy-consuming her slender form. She was a tadpole hair away from going full Sprite on the bird. And despite the difference in size that definitely favored the bird, my money was on my assistant.

Nobody did malicious like a Sprite.

"Sebille!"

"Hey," a high-pitched, friendly voice said from the door.

Sebille's gaze jerked toward Maude as the smiling teen came through the door, cuddling Mr. Slimy against her belly. "How's it going in here? Can I get you something to eat? We have cookies. I made them myself."

Sebille let her magic bleed away, but she threw the snotty bird a warning glance as I stood. "Cookies sound great. Sebille and I will help. She makes a mean cup of tea."

I was pretty sure the smile on Maude's face was a tiny bit smug as we fell in behind her and headed for the kitchen.

She'd played that one like a pro.

The kitchen was archaic and modern at the same time. Massive stainless-steel appliances anchored the extensive cabinetry in the room, and crisp white curtains fluttered at the windows. The space was massive, big enough to have served a hundred people on a daily basis if the castle had ever been used like a fortress, as I suspected it once had.

The floor consisted of rough, dark stone, cut in massive rectangles. The walls were painted white. There were more of the strange rugs covered in rune symbols that I'd noticed in other parts of the house. They softened the stone in the usual spots, such as in front of the sink and underneath a long, granite table with eight chairs.

The cabinets were crafted of dark wood, with pebbled glass inserts in the doors, and there was a massive concrete farm sink beneath a large window overlooking the grassy back yard.

Just the fact that Madeline Quilleran *had* a back yard in the middle of the Enchanted Forest proved how powerful she was. Especially since the whole thing moved around on a regular basis, to keep her location secret.

I dropped into a chair at the oversized table, scanning a look down its length, past a candelabra that had probably been made during the thirteenth century, and to the wide bay window that wrapped around the opposite end. "How have you been, Maude. Are you happy here?"

"It's okay. There's lots to do and Aunt Maddie's tons of fun." The teen placed Mr. Slimy on the floor and went over to the massive sink to wash her hands.

Sebille snorted softly. "Tons of fun, huh?"

Maud tugged the lid off a frog-shaped cookie jar and pulled several oversized cookies from its wide depths. "I know she seems dire to you guys. But she's totally different with me."

"How are your experiments with Rustin's... problem coming?" I asked.

She shrugged. "We've isolated something in the frog that's interesting. I'm not sure what it means yet, but I'm encouraged."

I hadn't been expecting that. "Something in Slimy? What do you mean?"

Maude pointed to a cannister on the counter. "Tea stuff is in there."

Sebille opened the cannister and started pulling out tiny lidded pots, opening them and sniffing each with a grin. Apparently, the Sprite approved of the leaves the Quillerans had available. She liked to mix her own special blends from the loose tea. I could honestly say I'd never tasted a mix from Sebille that I didn't love.

Maude carried the plate of cookies over and put it in front of me, laying a pile of napkins next to it. "Slimy..." she grinned as if she thought the name was funny. She probably thought I'd named him that as a joke. I hadn't, of course. I named him Slimy because I thought frogs were slimy and nasty. Though, as I'd gotten used to having the little guy around, that had changed some. "He's benefiting from Rustin's presence in ways we hadn't expected."

I felt my eyes go round. "Benefitted?" I was flummoxed. "I hadn't expected him to be affected at all." Even as I said the words, I realized how stupid they were. Of course, he'd have been changed after being subjected to a dark magic spell that basically inserted a powerful witch into him. "Benefitted how?"

She pulled a napkin over and placed a cookie onto it, picking at the edges as she thought about my question. "Well, we expected him to become more intelligent from the connection. What we didn't expect was the change in his longevity."

Sebille placed tea in front of Maude and me. "He's going to have a longer life span?" She asked.

Maude nodded. "We're guessing he might live a normal human lifespan. Maybe even longer. He could live a few hundred years like a witch. We're just not sure yet."

I gulped, trying to swallow the sudden knot in my throat. I'd figured I'd have to babysit the squishy green thing for a few months, maybe a couple of years. But centuries? "Yikes," I murmured. I wasn't sure how I felt about that. Granted, I didn't wish death on the little guy. And when I thought about losing him, I did get an unexpected tightness in my chest. But centuries?

Maude nodded as Sebille dropped into a chair next to her with another cup of tea. "Amazing, huh?"

"More amazing than Sebille's eye-rolling muscles," I murmured, setting off said muscles in response.

Maude chewed for a moment, watching the frog hop around the kitchen.

"If he's smart...er..." I said. "Is there any chance I can potty train him? I'm tired of getting peed on."

Maude snickered. "I suppose so. But only if he wants to do it. You can't force him to pee on command. It has to be his idea."

Of course it did. Something told me I was doomed to centuries of getting peed on by the frog.

"Besides," Sebille added helpfully, "You'd have to teach him to sing the Magic Muffin song." She snickered.

I thought about this for a moment. "Can he sing?" I asked Maude.

I expected her to giggle, but she didn't. She shook her head, swallowing a bite of cookie. "I don't think so. But it *is* pretty cool that he's talking now."

11

INFESTED!

old the galloping seahorses. "Wait, what?" I stuttered out. "Talking? No. He's not..."

Maude fixed me with a look. "Don't tell me you haven't spoken to him?"

My lips flapped a few times, but no words dared fall through them. I glanced at Sebille and she shrugged, her focus on the huge chocolate chip cookie she was nibbling.

I saw no option other than to admit it. "No. I haven't talked to the frog. What did he say?"

Maude turned to the fat green form sitting on the chair next to her.

When had *that* happened? The last time I'd noticed him he'd been hopping around on the floor.

"Lots of stuff. Mostly that he hates his new house and that he wishes you'd quit letting the artifacts run rampant at Croakies." She flushed slightly, seeming to realize how that sounded. "I think he was just letting off a little steam."

She lifted her cup and sipped, hiding behind the pretty china as I glared over at the frog. "That fish tank cost me fifty dollars," I told the frog. "I thought you'd like it. You can see the whole place, the cool breezes coming through the door can't get to you, and I don't have to worry about somebody stepping on you by accident."

The frog looked back at me, throat swelling and deflating, gaze blank.

Maude turned to look at him. She snickered. "I know, right?"

I glowered at the little green traitor. "What's he saying about me?"

Maude cleared her throat, giving me a pitying look. "You can't hear him?"

"No." Heat filled my face. My own frog didn't want to talk to me. But he'd talk to a virtual stranger. I fought a sudden urge to remind him that Maude's family was responsible for dragging him from his peaceful pond and saddling him with a snarky ghost witch. "What kind of house would he like then?"

Maude looked at Mr. Slimy. He looked at me. Sebille snorted cookie out of her nose and hurried to clean it up with one of the paper napkins.

I turned my glower on her. "Don't tell me you can understand him too?"

"Of course. I can't believe you haven't heard him haranguing to be fed and stuff."

My eyes went wide. "That was him? I thought it was Rustin."

Maude and Sebille shared a look. "He does sound a little bit like Rustin," Maude said. Sebille nodded in agreement. "Must be a side effect of the bonding magic."

"Why won't he talk to me?" I asked, my feelings hurt.

"Because you don't want to hear him," Sebille said in her usual, cold, succinct way. "When you want to hear what he has to say, you will."

But I'd heard him before and I hadn't wanted to. Though, I'd thought it was Rustin. I stared at the frog and bit back the apology I wanted to give him. I'd tried to help him. I'd kept him safe, fed him, unplugged him from the sink when he'd fallen into the drain trying to catch a fly. I'd done everything I could to help. And all I got for my efforts was frog flak.

Dang ungrateful frog.

Footsteps sounded in the hall. We all turned to see Lea bouncing into the room, smiling. She was followed by a stern-faced Rustin.

"We think we've had a breakthrough," Lea told me. She dropped into a seat at the table and grabbed a cookie. "That lab is pure ice."

In my current grumpy state, I almost asked her if

it was cubed or crushed, but I pressed my lips together. It wasn't her fault my frog was an ingrate. "You know who magicked the youth cream?" I asked.

"Not *who*, exactly," Lea said, moaning as she tasted the cookie and giving Maude a thumbs up. "But *what*."

"Goblins," Rustin said with a grimace. "Nasty creatures."

I forgot to be mad at Slimy for a moment, excitement filling me. "Like the ones running the cosmetics company Queen Sindra mentioned?"

Lea nodded, patting Sebille's hand as if congratulating her for her mother's foresight.

Sebille rolled her eyes.

I glanced toward the door as Madeline stepped into the kitchen. Her long, black skirt swished against her ankles but her soft shoes were silent on the stone. Rasputin rode her shoulder, his unfriendly silver gaze locked on Sebille.

Something told me he wouldn't soon forget their little altercation. I knew the Sprite wouldn't either. She didn't take it well when someone called her a bug. Especially when that someone ate bugs on a regular basis.

I caught Madeline's gaze. "I hear you found our culprit?"

She shook her head. "No. There's definitely goblin magic in the sample." She frowned down at the plastic container. "But there's something else there, a residue of something ancient."

"Ancient like what?"

Her head snapped up. "I've seen this signature before. It has elements of youth magic Hebe once used."

"The goddess of youth?" Sebille asked. She shook her head. "Why would Hebe make a cream that kills older women?"

"She wouldn't," Madeline said, her gaze falling to mine. "But someone who'd stolen Hebe's essence might do it."

"Is that possible?" I asked.

"What do you think powered the fountain of youth?" Rasputin asked, snottily.

I felt my eyes go wide. "Could this be tied to the fountain?"

Madeline shrugged. "Impossible to say. But I'm guessing not. This feels like..." She frowned.

"Like what?" I finally asked when she fell into her thoughts.

"Like a trial run. I have nothing at all to back up that feeling," she hurried to add. "But my experience as a PTB tells me this isn't as straight-forward as we'd assumed."

"Speaking of that," I said. "I haven't gotten an order for this artifact, whatever it is. Do you think the system has failed again?"

She frowned. "I don't *want* to think that."

Neither did I. We'd all hoped the missing order for the coin artifact had been a one-off. A fluke. But there was apparently a poisonous, anti-aging artifact somewhere in Enchanted, and I hadn't been sent an order to deal with it. Something was very wrong.

Madeline lifted the container. "Mind if I keep this for a bit? There are a couple more tests I'd like to run on it."

How could I say no when she was being so civil? Everybody in the room knew she could just take the sample. I wouldn't be able to stop her. "Sure. You'll let me know if you figure something out?"

"Of course." She glanced toward the fat frog sitting at the table, her brows lowering. I thought she was going to yell at me for letting my frog sit at her table. Instead, she nodded, her yellow gaze sliding to me. "Your frog is hungry."

With that bombshell, she turned away and headed, presumably, back to her lab.

"He talked to her too?" Even to me, I sounded pathetic.

When Sebille patted me on the shoulder, I knew I'd fallen to the depths of wretchedness.

But I had a good excuse for my pitiable state. My frog liked everybody but me.

We returned to Croakies rather than go to see the goblins right away. I needed to do some research before I blundered into their lair. Make sure I knew what I was up against. Plus, I had to lick my wounds over Slimy. It wasn't every day one got dissed by one's frog.

It might take me a minute to learn how I felt about it.

I disengaged the locks and pushed the door open as Rustin and Sebille bickered behind me. It seemed the ghost witch hadn't appreciated having to sit in the back seat on the trip back from the forest. He'd called shotgun just a little too slow. Sebille was an old pro at the whole shotgun thing. He'd have to up his game to beat her.

"I don't know why you're giving me grief," Sebille told him unkindly. "You're not even a whole person. You could have floated outside the car if you'd wanted to. Your tether to the frog is extra-long now."

"I am too a whole person, Sprite. I'm just a little..." He seemed to be struggling for the right word.

I grinned. "Wispy?"

Sebille's snort followed me as I pushed the door open. I jolted to a stop on the threshold, getting a backside full of Sprite and ghost witch from my unexpected stop.

"Ugh!" Sebille said, taking a breath to let me

have it. The words never came. I felt her breath gush out as she took in the sight that had stopped me in my tracks.

"*Holy dragonfly pimples*," I muttered, my stomach twisting. "Sebille?"

"I swear I put it away."

Rustin snickered. "Bibbity Bobbity Boo!"

Bubbles floated through the air. Hordes of them. All iridescent and shiny and smelling of lavender soap. As I stood there looking around in horror, a particularly friendly bubble rose up from the soggy carpet and assailed my nose, happily popping to leave behind a cool, wet spot on my skin.

"Why?" I asked nobody in particular.

"It's what it does," Sebille answered unnecessarily.

I turned to fling a glare in her direction. "You left it out, didn't you? Just admit it."

"I swear on my mother's wings, I put it back on the shelf."

The shelves in the artifact library were infused with a spell to hold and mitigate the magic of the artifacts, releasing them only if I recalled them with my magic or someone who had permission to manage them took them down.

I definitely hadn't released the wand from the shelves. That left Sebille.

"Alligator pinkie swear," she told me, her green eyes wide.

"Alligators don't have pinkies," Rustin said, grinning widely.

"This isn't funny, Rustin!" I told him with some heat. "Look at the books."

All three of us turned to stare at the dripping bookshelves, bubbles still dancing over the saturated tomes and water sliding down to puddle in the carpet.

"The thing seems to have misfired," Sebille said.

"Ya think?" I said a bit too loudly. Then I groaned, stepping into the store. My shoes squelched over the saturated rug, soapy water seeping between my toes.

Anger filled me at the destruction. My bad mood was invigorated by frustration with Sebille, the artifact, and the terrible, bad, awful day I'd had.

I threw out my keeper magic and heard a soft, happy whistling sound wind toward us from the artifact library. The door between the two spaces was ajar and it shouldn't have been. My cat must have left it open again.

I added Wicked to the list of friends and things I was mad at.

The happy whistling came closer until it burst upon the air on the sparkling, star-shaped heels of Cinderella's wand, the small, pastel-hued length of wood and magic dancing into Croakies with a song in its heart and destruction at its tip.

It skidded to a stop in front of us, dipping as if

giving us a curtsy, and then tilting sideways as my magic found it and tugged it toward my outstretched hand.

The wand fought the grasp of my magic, sending a pretty burst of bubbles into the air as it tried to get away.

I stepped closer, determined to grab the pesky little wand and stick it in the toxic artifact vault where it apparently belonged.

But the wand was determined not to be corralled. It tipped, the dangerous end shooting up to point right at us, and a burst of fire-hose strength water and soap shot out of it, sending me flying backward to bash into Sebille and Rustin.

The ghost witch gave a shout of discomfort as my assistant and I fell right through him and slammed into the door.

Then, happy tune rising once again from its magical tip, the jovial wand danced back through the door and disappeared, slamming it in its wake.

My cell phone rang.

I shoved to my feet, pushing soapy water out of my face as I dug in the soggy pocket of my jeans for my phone. "It's Grym." I glanced to my friends. "Can you guys corral that thing and put it into the vault?"

Sebille didn't even bother responding. She shoved a soapy, drenched red braid off her face and stalked toward the door, growling deep in her throat.

I didn't envy that stupid wand. Especially when

the ghost witch shot after her, a murderous look in his gaze.

"Hey, Grym," I said, wiping soap off my mouth with my shoulder. "I think we might have some information on the youth cream case."

A beat of silence met my statement. I pulled the phone away, looking at the screen to make sure it hadn't disconnected. If that stupid wand had broken my phone...

"Naida?"

I blinked. It wasn't Grym. It sounded like a kid. "Who is this?"

The kid cleared his throat, coughing wetly. "It's me, Naida. Grym. I think I'm running out of time. We need to figure out who made that cream and find out if there's a way to reverse it."

The dividing door flew open and Wicked shot through, yowling pitifully. He was soaking wet and trailing bubbles as he shot across the store and into his hidey-hole beneath the counter.

The wand shot through after him. Jerked to a stop in the air and spun in one direction then the other, seemingly looking for my cat.

"Grym, you sound really young," I told him frowning.

Sebille and Rustin burst through the door. Sebille threw herself into the air and made a grab for the wand. It shot straight toward the ceiling and skittered across, leaving a wet, soapy trail on the plaster as it headed for the door.

I gestured wildly toward the window, afraid it would blast through like the staff.

Rustin went high and Sebille went low. They cut the wand off at the wall, and it bolted in my direction.

Grym coughed again. He sounded terrible. "You should see me."

I really didn't want to. It would make it all too real. My friend was in danger.

"I look like a twelve-year-old. But that's not the worst of it. I think my body is fighting the rapid change. My systems feel like they're shutting down."

My hand snaked out and I grabbed the wand, sending a jolt of keeper magic into the thing as it fought to escape.

Grym's voice was filled with fear. I didn't like the sound. Grym was a gargoyle. He was big and strong, and I'd watched him stand up to a dragon. He couldn't be taken down by beauty cream.

Could he?

Sebille grabbed the artifact from my hand and slipped it quickly into a quelling bag, sealing the top with her magic.

I sagged downward, the starch suddenly leaving my knees as I realized how much danger my friend was in. "I'm going to get to the bottom of this, Grym,"

I told him. "I promise. But you need to hang in there."

Silence pulsed through the phone lines, threaded through by a wheezing sound I hoped wasn't Grym's breathing. Unfortunately, I was pretty sure it was.

"Hurry, Naida."

He disconnected. I stumbled backward, dropping into the nearest chair as my legs turned to jelly.

"Naida?"

I looked up to find Rustin hovering nearby, his expression worried. "Are you okay?"

I looked down at my hands. They were shaking. Grym was in terrible danger. I couldn't stop my mind from sliding back to those horrible lumps of tissue on the chairs in Celia Pepper's home. How long before Grym became like those poor women? "We need to find that artifact," I told the ghost witch.

Sebille returned, her expression dark. "That stupid cat is going to the moon."

I forced my mind out of its dark place and glanced up. "Why? What did he do now?"

"The shelves are a mess back there. Stuff all over the floor. It's no wonder the wand was in here wreaking havoc." She frowned down at me. "You need to lock him in your apartment when you're gone."

I shook my head. "I'm not locking Mr. Wicked up," I told my assistant. "What makes you think he's responsible for the artifacts being off the shelf. Maybe Cinderella's wand tidied the shelves and shoved them off."

Sebille gave me her patented "You're an idiot" look. "That's not how the wand works, Keeper."

I swung my arm around the bookstore, seeing the devastation anew and feeling tears burning my eyes. "This isn't how it's supposed to work, either, Sebille."

She shrugged. "You have a point. But I saw him back there, burrowing around in the artifacts. Him and his little sister."

I felt my eyes go wide. "Hex is here?" I wondered if Lea knew her cat was in the library. She hadn't called to tell me the cat was coming.

The front door opened and my friend came through, her eyes going wide at the sight. "Oh no, Naida. Not again."

I wasn't sure if she was referring to the earlier devastation caused by Maleficent's wayward staff, or the wreckage caused by Felicity Quilleran when she'd visited the store a few weeks ago looking for Mr. Slimy and his resident ghost witch.

Lea stepped inside and her foot squished in the saturated carpet. I bit my lip to keep from grinning. She was wearing a fuzzy pink onesie and her long, blonde hair was twisted up on top of her head in a messy ponytail. "What in the... Are those bubbles?"

I sighed. "Long story. Did you know Hex was here?"

She expelled a huge sigh. "Thank the goddess. I couldn't find her anywhere. I was starting to panic."

"Why are you dressed like a giant infant?" Sebille asked in a tone filled with disgust.

Lea looked down at herself, running her hands over the fuzzy belly of her suit. "These are my PJs. It gets cold in the apartment over the shop at night."

Sebille snorted out a laugh, and I glared at her. "I seem to remember seeing you in a striped onesie when you stayed with me."

She flushed.

"Which reminds me. Where...?"

"Why are you here in your PJs?" Sebille asked Lea, cutting me off with a quick sideways glance.

"I was heading downstairs to make myself some hot chocolate when I realized Hex was missing. I searched the apartment, the shop, and the greenhouse."

"How did she get into Croakies?" I mused aloud. "We've been gone for a couple of hours."

Lea sighed. "I wasn't going to tell you this but..."

Whatever it was, she wouldn't catch my eye. Apparently, I wasn't going to like it. I braced for whatever she was going to tell me, thinking unhappily that everyone and everything around me seemed to be changing at an uncomfortable rate of speed.

"...through the mirror."

I blinked, bringing myself out of my thoughts in time to catch her last words. I didn't need her to repeat it. I had a feeling I already knew what she'd said. "Hex came through the standing mirror in the library?"

Lea bit her bottom lip, nodding. "I'm sorry, Naida. I bespelled the mirror in the shop to keep her from using it, but she must have found another mirror."

"Or used standing water," Sebille added helpfully. "Those little monsters are fully capable of using any scrying object to travel."

I pounded my thighs with my fists. "*Butterfly halitosis!* You knew, Sebille? And you didn't tell me?"

She shrugged her bony shoulders, totally unconcerned with my anger. "I didn't know for sure. But it makes sense."

I shook my head, losing patience with the conversation. "Whatever. We have bigger problems to deal with right now." I looked at Lea. "I'll shroud the mirror until we can figure out how to stop, or at least limit them from traveling around."

Lea nodded.

"In the meantime, I need your help. Grym's in trouble." I quickly laid out Grym's failing health and regressive physical state. "At the rate he's deteriorating, I'm worried he doesn't have more than a couple of days before this youth magic takes him completely down." I grimaced at the euphemism, but I couldn't bring myself to say the word, "death" in relationship to Grym.

Lea thought about the problem for a moment, her agile mind clearly working it through. Finally, she nodded. "I feel confident that, between Madeline and me, we'll come up with a reversal spell soon..."

"He doesn't have much tim..."

She put up a hand to stop me. "But for now, I have a simple fix."

Hope flared in my chest. "What is it?"

"Tell Grym to take his magical form. I doubt the magic will work the same way in his gargoyle form. If nothing else it should be greatly slowed down."

"But what if it speeds it up?" Rustin asked.

All eyes turned to him. He'd been so quiet, I'd forgotten he was there.

"Is that a possibility?" I asked.

Rustin shrugged, his gaze sliding to Lea's.

She finally sighed. "A small one, but, yes. Magic is unpredictable at best. And since we don't know the underpinnings of the youth spell, there's no way to know for sure."

I felt hope crash around my feet.

"Tell him, Naida," Sebille said, her voice matter of fact. "Let him decide if it's worth the risk."

I thought about it another minute and then

sighed. "You're right. It's not our decision. It's his. I'll call him back."

Rustin's wispy form rustled closer. I looked up.

"There's something else," he told me.

And judging by his expression, it wasn't good. "What?"

He held a wispy palm in front of my nose. Cool, ozone-flavored air drifted to my nostrils as the translucent form of his hand stopped mere inches from my face. I squinted down at it, seeing a small pile of something black and sparkly in the center.

A scent like spent matches filtered through the ozone smell. "What is that?"

Lea bent over his hand too, reaching a finger toward the black stuff. She sighed, her gaze lifting to Rustin's. "I'm afraid it's not good news."

Rancid whale blubber. Of course it wasn't.

"Croakies is infested."

I frowned. "Infested? With what? Mice?"

Sebille clapped her hands with glee. "Please tell me Cinderella's magic mice coachmen are here? Please, please, please?"

We all looked at her like she'd sprouted a triangular pink nose and whiskers herself.

"Um, disturbing on so many levels," Lea said, "but no. I'm afraid you have a bad case of..."

"Hobgoblins," Rustin finished. "You have a hobgoblin infestation."

12

BLEEP THE BLOODY BUBBLES!

"But how!" I squealed, my gaze scouring the floor as I scratched suddenly itchy skin. "Why? Where could it have come from?"

Rustin opened his hand and let the dust fall. It expired in a puff of smoke before it hit the carpet. "*How* is the big question. *Why* is obvious. This place is heaven on earth for a prankster. But the consequences, as we've already seen, can be deadly."

Lea's eyes went wide. "You think somebody brought it here on purpose?"

"The timing is a bit suspicious, don't you think?" he told my friend.

Yes, it was. Very suspicious. "Somebody's trying to keep me off balance to make sure I don't find that youth artifact."

He inclined his chin. "That seems logical."

I started pacing the book store, my shoes

squishing loudly in the soapy, wet carpet. "This is bad. Really bad. If that things finds its way into the toxic magic vault..."

"It won't," Sebille said.

I stopped pacing, looking at her. "Do you know something you're not telling us?"

"No. I'm just saying, that vault is impervious to everything. Not so much as a cockroach can get in there."

"Unless you need to open it for some reason," Rustin said, his gaze flying to mine. "Like you did when you put the staff away."

"Goblin boogers!" I shouted. We all turned on our heels and started running for the vault. It wasn't until we reached the large, gray metal door situated in the deepest, darkest corner of the huge space that I realized we might be playing right into the thing's hands.

I turned to look at Lea and Rustin. "Can you guys put a barrier around this door? I don't want anything to get in or out of the vault while it's open."

They nodded and, a moment later, the air around us thickened, distorting the figures of Sebille and Rustin standing a few feet away through a glossy haze.

I nodded to Sebille.

She tugged a chain from under her dress. The key hanging from the chain was shaped like a thumbprint. I had no idea whose print it was, I assumed Bandy Joe's since he'd been the very first KoA to run Croakies. Sebille pressed the key into a special indentation on the smooth door and green light flared as the key synced with the metal. There was a beat of silence before the internal workings of the door started to rumble and click.

A moment later, the door shimmered with a harsh orange light. The opening quivered like heat over asphalt and thinned to a barrier Sebille and I could pass through, but nothing inside the vault would be able to penetrate.

It took us only a few minutes to determine that everything was as it should be inside the vault. Fortunately, we only had a handful of artifacts at Croakies that were considered dangerous enough to be enclosed inside the vault.

There was Maleficent's staff, of course, a small purse that made gold coins, the Evil Queen's magic mirror, shrouded for extra protection, a small bottle of love potion that made the victim kill to protect his or her loved one, and a few other items that hadn't moved since I'd taken over being the KoA at Croakies.

Everything seemed as it should. There were no hobgoblins flitting around the vault.

When we passed back out through the shimmering portal, the orange light oozed back into the door and it became solid again. As we walked away, we could hear the rumble of the inner workings settling back into place.

"Nothing?" Lea asked, chewing her bottom lip.

"No, thank the goddess," I told them. "Everything's in place."

Lea nodded, expelling a long breath. "Well, that's one scare averted. I'll just grab my cat and get out of your way." She started to turn away and stopped. "Unless you need help cleaning up the mess in the store?"

"No. But thanks. We've got this." I looked at Sebille.

"I'll get started drying the books," she said, marching off toward the front of the building.

I glanced around. "Did anybody see the cats on our way through the library?"

Rustin shook his head. "No. I'll go help Sebille with the store."

"Thank you!" I called out to him as he floated quickly away.

I dropped my arm around Lea's shoulders. "I guess you and I will have to find the little monsters."

"I can do it if you need to go help up front."

I snorted out a laugh. "Do you really think I'd rather go face that mess than spend time on a treasure hunt with two adorable cats at the end of the rainbow?"

She barked out a laugh. "Silly me."

Unfortunately, we'd gotten no closer to finding

the little minxes after an hour of searching. We'd heard lots of snuffling and clawing sounds, but when we followed the noise to the spot where we thought we'd heard the cats, they were nowhere to be found.

Neither cat was coming when we called either, which wasn't all that unusual since they *were* cats and not dogs...but despite that, I was getting worried.

We ended at the front of the library, standing near Shakespeare's desk. My gaze fell on the standing mirror we used to communicate with other magic users and, occasionally, for scrying or traveling.

I had a sudden worry that Wicked and Hex had gone through the mirror.

Lea must have had the same thought, she reached out and clasped my hand in a hard, icy grip. "Naida?"

"They wouldn't have," I said, though I wasn't entirely sure I was right.

"But if they did. How would we get them back?"

I had no idea. "If they went in there, they'll come back. They're probably better at magic than either of us." My voice was firm, but doubt made my throat dry. I swallowed hard against the panic.

Worst case scenario, Madeline might be able to help us get the cats back. But how did we know if they were in danger? Waiting to find out if they returned on their own suddenly seemed too risky.

My gaze slid to the desk and I had an idea. "Okay, let's think this through, I told her. I'm guessing, knowing those two, that they were in here looking for the hobgoblin, right?"

Lea nodded, frowning. "That seems the most logical reason. Hex has never snuck away before. She must have had a good reason."

I had my own thoughts on that, but I kept them to myself. Mr. Wicked sometimes thought finding the perfect ray of sunlight was a good reason to shove valuable artifacts to the floor of the library. Their sense of the appropriate didn't exactly match ours.

"So all we need to do is find that hobgoblin and we should find the cats."

She made a face that looked like she had a gas bubble. "That's not going to be easy in this place. There's at least an acre of space, filled to the ceiling with shelves and stuff. That thing could be hiding anywhere."

She wasn't wrong.

"Which is why we're going to get some help."

I sat down in the chair in front of Shakespeare's desk, placing my palms on the antique leather blotter in the center. The hand-tooled leather looked like a book bearing the Shakespeare family sigil, the family motto in blurred gold letters along the spine. *Non Sanz Droict*. Not without Right.

Fortunately, as the Keeper of the Artifacts, I

had the right to use the powerful artifact. "Show me a guide to finding hobgoblins," I asked the desk.

The leather warmed and moved beneath my touch as the artifact searched for the perfect reference volume. After a few endless moments, a bright light flashed above the desk and a book covered in red cloth floated on the air before me.

I reached for it and read the title engraved across the front. "*Hobgoblins and other Pesky Vermin.*"

Lea tugged a chair over next to me and sat down, only to shoot back to her feet with a shriek a moment later.

I didn't need to look at the chair she shoved angrily away to know she'd accidentally taken a seat in Casanova's chair.

"Somebody needs to castrate that stupid thing," she groused, causing the chair to leap into the air and hit the ground hard, its legs scooting rapidly along the floor as the chair disappeared into the stacks of artifacts.

I chuckled. "You said the magic words. Hopefully, it won't show up again for a while."

Lea harrumphed, still too irritated to laugh. Rather than trying to sit again, she stood over me and watched as I opened the ancient volume. The sour stench of old paper and book mold wafted upward as I turned to the index in the front.

We both shrieked in surprise as a face oozed

through the paper and rose into the air, a scary smile stretched across its surface.

I slammed the book closed and looked at the author's name written across the front cover.

Of course.

Doctor Mortimus Osvald.

The doctor and I had danced together before, when I'd been looking for a soul-stealing artifact. With a grimace, I stood up and looked at Lea. "If we're going to deal with Osvald, I think I'm going to need some tea."

I sat down at the table with a steaming cup of tea. Lea sat across from me, her gaze sliding nervously toward the book. "What's wrong with this Oswald guy?" she asked.

"Osvald," I corrected. I grimaced as the tea hit my tongue, way too herbal-ly tasting and scorching hot. I really wished I could brew tea like Sebille. She truly was tea-talented. "He's just odd and annoying."

I set my tea down and shoved it away, looking at Lea. "Ready?"

She frowned. "I'm not sure..."

I opened the book. Nothing happened for a moment. Finally, a nose and a pair of eyes oozed upward from the yellowed paper. The black eyes blinked and then the lips eased into view. "Is it safe?"

Guilt slid through me. I'd been kind of abrupt closing the book before. "Yeah. Sorry about that, Doctor Osvald. I had a...an emergency."

He eased upward, his head rising above the page and circling to take in the surrounding area. The dark brown hair was still unkempt, still clinging to his heavily veined neck, and his black eyes still seemed to follow me no matter how I moved.

Doctor Osvald looked like an evil character from a Grimm's Fairytale. I didn't believe the man was malevolent. However, the jury was still out on my second thought...that he was slightly insane.

As before, he addressed me with a smile, his full lips looking cracked and dry in his ruddy face. "Welcome to my comprehensive volume of Hobgoblins and Other Pesky Vermin. Would you like to read through the text on your own, or shall I guide you through the text and footnotes?"

I glanced at Lea and she shrugged, sipping her tea. She didn't grimace so either my horrible attempt at tea had numbed her palate completely, or she was used to me making horrible tea.

I decided it would be faster for him to give us the high points. "Your guidance, please."

Osvald inclined his shaggy head. "Excellent. Where shall we start?"

"I've been infested by a hobgoblin."

Osvald's head seemed to shudder, his eyes rolling back in his head.

My pulse spiked. Were the little pranksters really that bad? I swallowed hard. "Can you help me find it?"

His eyes opened and he gave me that tight, terrifying smile again. "Of course. That's why I'm here." He frowned. "Well, actually I'm here because a warlock bound me to my library of books and I can't escape until a thousand people ask for my help."

I felt my face fall. "Oh." That was so sad.

Then he grinned. "Gotcha."

"Hey," I said. "That was mean. I was feeling sorry for you."

He laughed. "I just thought you should know what you were in for. Hobgoblins are skilled at playing the victim. They're wretched little actors who take great pleasure in creating chaos wherever they go."

"Fiddling frog farts," I murmured.

He nodded in agreement. "Hobgoblins are the cockroaches of the magical world. They tend to hide inside walls and underneath floors. They're happiest within the bones of a structure and have been known to set up nests and grow large families if left alone in a place for long enough."

Lea gave me an "Oh, shirt!" look, and I let my eyes go wide.

"We need to find it before it gets to that," I told Osvald.

"There's only one sure-fire way to rid yourself of the little pests."

I sat closer. "I'm listening."

He nodded. "Burn the whole place to the ground."

I sat there, blinking, sure he was tweaking me again. Unfortunately, Osvald stared back at me, his scary black eyes filled with sincerity.

"I can't burn Croakies down," I told him, my voice breaking a bit as hysteria tightened my chest.

"That's unfortunate," Osvald said.

"Unfortunate!" I said, my voice slightly screechy. "It's not unfortunate. This is my home. I have untold magic housed within these walls. It's my job to take care of all of it. I can't just burn it down."

Osvald's gaze grew slightly concerned by my screeching. He looked around the room, possibly searching for an exit. But he was stuck there, hovering over the apparently useless pages of his stupid book.

"You need to help me. This book..." I stabbed my finger against the Chapter heading on the first page. "This says, *How to Locate and Expel a Hobgoblin.* There has to be a way that doesn't destroy everything."

Osvald's mouth came open and his eyes skimmed to Lea, a pleading light in them.

My friend leaned closer, her gaze filled with tension. "You. Will. Help."

Fire sparked in her pretty gaze, magic lighting her face with golden power. It was a very scary and effective sight. I'd seen her use it before to make an impression.

It seemed to work especially well on the book squatter. If he'd had hands, I'm pretty sure he'd have raised them in defense. "All right, you two." His bookish aristocratic accent succumbed to a Cockney twang as he bobbled on the air in front of us. "I do have some things you can try."

"Good." I gave Lea a smile and she sat back, sipping her tea and making a face as she plucked an errant hunk of leaf from her tongue.

I grimaced apologetically.

"Start talking," I told the so-called Hobgoblin expert.

"As I said, the hobgoblin enjoys the structure of a building. You can break up all the walls..."

"Nope. Next," I interrupted.

He cleared his throat. "Yes, well. Sometimes an electrical current coursing through the walls will..."

"Uh, uh," I said.

He sighed. "A carefully pinpointed explosion..."

I flicked his nose, sending him shooting backward on a yelp of surprise.

"I say!"

Lea snorted out a laugh. "You didn't even feel that."

"No, but it was alarming."

"Not nearly as alarming as your suggestions have been so far," I groused.

He huffed out a breath. "There is one thing, but it's highly experimental."

"Does it destroy the building?"

"Destroy? Er, no, but..."

"Then it's just the ticket. What is it?"

"Cleanse the space with burning sage. The sage will hypnotize and draw the hobgoblin out of the walls. Then you must use a magic trap to capture him."

"A magic trap?" I asked, glancing at Lea.

She shook her head.

"Like you'd trap a demon or a fallen angel," Osvald clarified unhelpfully.

I lifted my brows. Did he really think Lea and I regularly trapped celestial beings?

"Do you mean a pentacle?" Lea asked.

Osvald's lips pressed together. "I don't know the specifics. I only know you must use a magic trap. May I leave now? I've had just about as much fun as I care to have today."

I lifted the cover and prepared to close the book, hesitating as his thick brows lifted in worry. "Sorry. I'm a little upset about all this."

He harrumphed. "I'd be grateful if you never opened this book again."

Feeling bad, I closed the cover gently and let

Doctor Osvald retreat to the safety of wherever he went.

I glanced at Lea. "Any ideas about a magic trap?"

She shook her head, pushing to her feet. "I'll go do some research." She started out and then stopped, her gaze sliding to the mirror in my bathroom across the room. "You'll let me know if they show up...?"

Sadness filled me as I followed her line of sight.

The kittens.

I nodded, sighing as she left. I was suddenly so tired. I had so many problems to solve and I didn't seem to be making headway into any of them.

13

THE HOBGOBLIN OF LITTLE MINDS...

I tossed and turned all night, dreaming about Mr. Wicked and imagining all sorts of horrible things that might be happening to him and Hex on their little adventure. My biggest concern was that Wicked had used the Book of Pages to travel somewhere. He seemed to have a direct conduit to the keeper tool. It responded to him much more readily than it ever had for me. And I could definitely see him using it if there was something he wanted to do.

I woke well before the sun rose, my gaze sliding to the empty, Wicked-shaped dip in the pillow. My hand slipped over the indentation, tears burning in my gaze.

It had occurred to me at some point in the night that Wicked might have been taken. But the fact that Hex was missing too pointed strongly toward the probability that they were having an adventure.

"Turtle toes!" I muttered, feeling helpless and inept.

The niggling doubt that they were in danger, possibly because of something I'd done...or hadn't done...wouldn't leave me alone.

I needed to start solving problems soon, or I was going to lose too many people I cared about. It was just a miracle the youth magic hadn't struck again. That realization made me wonder if it hadn't been specifically targeted toward the book club for some reason. And that thought brought forward a new fear, along with an old one.

Were Mrs. Foxladle and Franny Clauss in danger? Or, almost worse, were they the perpetrators of the crime themselves?

At four-thirty AM, I finally gave up and climbed out of bed. After singing the Make Me a Magic Muffin song, I burnt some tea and checked my phone. I'd texted Grym the night before to tell him what Lea had said about taking his gargoyle form to slow down the progression.

He'd finally texted me back a couple of hours later. His message was brief. *Thanks. Cosmetics plant in the morning?*

I texted back my agreement and made a note to call him later to find out if changing to his super-normal form had helped.

I carried my tea downstairs, intending to give the library and bookstore another thorough look for the two cats.

My eyes went wide as I stepped off the bottom stair and saw the shrouded, standing mirror wobbling on its rickety legs, a persistent dinging sound emanating from under the black fabric I'd shrouded it with.

I ran over and yanked off the shroud without thinking, hoping it was Wicked and Hex trying to come through, and my eyes went wide.

The face staring back at me was narrow and pale, with a sharp chin, made even sharper by the dark blond goatee speckling the pink skin. The man wore a dark suit coat with rounded lapels and a bowler hat. His thin mustache twitched beneath his nose as he looked at me, making him look like a mouse sizing up a predator. "Miss Griffith?"

I frowned at the plaque on the pale wood desk behind which he was seated, recognizing the sigil of the Société of Dire Magic. "Yes."

He inclined the sharp chin, pale blue eyes dipping for a beat as he plucked a sheet of paper off the top of the desk. "I'm Rogers from the SDM." He stopped, seeming to wait for my response.

My frown deepened. "Okay. What's this about?"

His gaze dipped to the paper in his hands. "I'm responding to a report that you've lost control of not one but two dangerous artifacts. The Société is considering recalling you as Keeper until you can be properly re-trained."

My mouth fell open and I blinked rapidly, my stomach twisting with alarm. "What report?"

I realized as soon as the words escaped my lips that I'd glommed onto the least important part of the problem, but I couldn't seem to help myself. I wanted to know who'd ratted me out.

"That's not important, Miss Griffith..."

"It is to me."

His lips pressed together and his brows lifted, not very effective at showing his displeasure since they were so light I could barely see them. "Do you have any idea how much trouble you're in, Miss Griffith?"

"No, I don't. That's mostly because this is the first time I'm hearing about this. I've done a good job as keeper since having the job dumped on me without adequate training..."

His lips curved upward as I realized my mistake and hurried to try to correct it. "But I've trained myself..."

His smile widened. "That's obvious, Miss G..."

"Please call me Keeper, it is my title and I've earned it."

The smile slid away, the pale gaze darkening with pique. "This was a courtesy call to inform you that I will be closely monitoring the situation. Good day, Miss Griffith."

The image in the mirror disappeared, turning the glass dark for a moment before the charcoal smoke of the communication magic eased away.

I stood staring at the empty glass for a long moment, feeling sick to my stomach and terrified at the same time.

The Société couldn't take my job away from me... could they? I just wasn't sure. And since I was the only Keeper of the Artifacts in my dimension, there was nobody I could ask. "Troll boogers!" I exclaimed, beginning to pace. What was I going to do?

Everything was upside down and backward and I seemed unable to figure out how to fix any of it. Maybe the Société was right. Maybe I should be recalled for training.

I sighed, swiping angrily at the tears sliding down my cheeks. I could really use Mr. Wicked right about now. Cuddling with him always made me feel better.

Hello?

I jerked to a stop, thinking at first that someone was in the library with me. I looked around, trying to find the source of the voice.

Holy hog feathers! the voice said. *Are you deaf?*

I glanced toward the tallest shelf and the parrot perched atop Blackbeard's sword, frowning. "Not right now, SB. I'm busy."

SB? Do I look like a parrot to you? Holy horned

housefly, you have got to be the thickest creature I've ever met.

"Yes, you do look..." I stopped, realizing the parrot's head was down, his chest moving rhythmically as if he were sleeping. "SB?"

The parrot's head stayed down.

I think that little guy dosed him with something, the voice said. *After he put me up here.*

Little guy? I realized after hearing more of it, that the voice definitely didn't sound like SB's. But then, who was it?

Maude Quilleran's declaration perked in my mind. *No, it couldn't be.* "Mr. Slimy?"

Of course it's me. Who else would it be? Can you get me down from here, please? I have vertigo and I've been stuck here all night. Which reminds me, has anybody ever told you that you sleep like the dead?

I hurried over to the shelf and looked up. Sure enough, huddled against the parrot was a squishy green body. "What are you doing with the parrot? I didn't think you even liked him."

I was cold, the frog said, sounding slightly embarrassed.

I lifted my hand to send my keeper magics out but he hopped toward the edge, then turned and hopped quickly back. *No! Please don't use that magic stuff to fly me down there, it terrifies me.*

I wrinkled up my face. "Magic terrifies you? But you're a magical frog." I glanced around, looking for the sliding ladder. Of course it was at the far end of the shelves.

What can I tell you? I'm complex.

I snorted out a laugh. "Hold on, I'm getting the ladder."

A moment later, when I had him in my hands, I noticed the fine shiver of his pudgy form. "You are cold. Come on, I'll put you under the heat lamp in your terrarium."

I hate that place, he told me in a petulant tone.

"In my defense, I didn't know you hated it until recently. We'll come up with something else for you, I promise. But right now you need the warmth of that lamp."

He didn't disagree. I settled him on the flat rock inside his fish tank and turned on the lamp. "I'm going to cover you up too. That will keep the heat inside the tank."

Whatever, he responded morosely.

I laid the flannel cloth I'd been using to tuck him in for the night over the glass tank and went to get the bag of crickets from the cabinet under the register. I dumped a few into the container and covered it back up. "I have to make a phone call, then I'll be back. Eat up."

He snagged the first cricket before I'd even laid the flannel back over the container.

I looked at the clock, seeing it was after five in the morning. Still early. But LA started her days before dawn and I thought she might be awake and doing her chores. If anyone might know how to help me catch a hobgoblin it would be her or her witch.

LA answered on the third ring, sounding breathless and cheerful. "Hey, Naida! What's up?"

"I'm sorry to call so early."

"No, that's fine. I was just feeding the cats." She had a smile in her voice. "Glyph says hi."

Glyph was Mr. Wicked and Hex's littermate. I'd been thrilled when LA had decided to keep him. Her witch, Deg and friend Mandy who was also a witch had kept the last two kittens from the litter.

"We need to come down for a visit soon." A sad feeling tightened my chest at the reminder that I was currently missing a cat.

"You do! That would be fun."

I shoved my worries away, focusing on the reason for my call. "I was wondering if you'd had any experience with hobgoblins."

She groaned softly. "Oh no. Are you infested?"

"Apparently I am."

"Well, the good news is that they mostly just prank you. They're not malicious or especially dangerous. Unfortunately, in your case even a prank can turn dangerous."

I agreed, telling her about the released staff and wand. Though the wand hadn't physically harmed anybody, it could have destroyed a lot of valuable magical artifacts and reference books.

"You need to find the little guy fast," LA told me. "I can ask Deg and do some research. But off the top of my head, you'll need a magic trap."

Excitement flared. "Yes! That's what Doctor Osvald said too. But Lea and I weren't exactly sure what he meant. Apparently, there are a lot of spells for trapping. Will any of them work?"

"It's not a spell," LA said. "Well, not only a spell. It's an artifact. You actually might have one on the shelves."

Hope grew. "What does it look like?"

LA described it to me and hope puddled around my feet like a bride's gown on her wedding night. "I don't have one of those. Fairy farts!"

LA chuckled. "You don't by any chance know a giant, do you?" Her tone of voice made it clear she expected me to say no.

"I do! Why?"

"Giants almost always have magic traps because, like at Croakies, hobgoblins can do a lot of damage in a giant's home artifact. Ask your giant if he has a trap you can borrow. Then all you need is the frosted chocolate brownie."

"What's that now?"

She laughed. "You bait the trap with the brownie. Hobgoblins are helpless against frosted brownies."

Wasn't everybody? "You've saved my life," I told my friend. "Thank you!"

She laughed. "No problem. Is there anything else I can help with?"

The way she asked made me wonder if she knew about my trouble with the SDM. "You heard?"

She sighed. "Unfortunately. It hit the web and all of Illusion City has probably heard by now."

The web she was referring to wasn't the one most people would probably be thinking about. It was a supernormal network for magic users in Illusion City that helps the council keep track of supernormals in case of problems or danger. The network was fed by the magic energy of everyone in the city and was almost impermeable to being hacked. Almost. As long as I'd known LA it had only been breached once, with deadly consequences.

"You'll be okay," LA told me. "The SDM occasionally throws its weight around as an example to magic users to tow the line. If they try to discipline you, I'd be happy to serve as a witness for your defense. I'm sure Deg would too. Your friends won't let them railroad you, Naida."

I felt marginally better. Although her mention of discipline made my stomach knot. The SDM's "disciplines" were legendary for their harshness. "There is one more thing..." I hated to let her know Wicked was missing, but I was so worried about him. Maybe LA would have some insights for me. I told her about the cats.

"They're probably looking for the hobgoblin,"

she said very reasonably. "Cats are drawn to hobgoblins for obvious reasons."

"But neither Lea nor I have seen them since early yesterday. It's not like Wicked to stay away this long."

Silence filled the line as I presumed she gave my concern some thought. "You're right. This is more than that. What else do you have going on right now?"

"Other than dealing with the fallout from the hobgoblin, there's my talking frog."

LA laughed. "Seriously? Fun!"

"Yeah," I smiled. "It is kind of cool. I'll tell you all about it when we come for a visit. But the big thing, the thing that's gotten me into trouble with the Société is the youth magic artifact. If I don't find it soon, I'm going to lose a new friend and possibly more unsuspecting people to its effects."

"There are no leads?"

"Not much, no. The strangest thing is that the cream which apparently shrunk those poor people down to their very beginnings wasn't found at either scene. The killer has to be returning to take it away."

"And nobody's seen him or her leaving?"

I thought about the salesman boyfriend who was our only real lead. "There's one guy. Detective Grym and I are going to check him out this morning." If Grym wasn't too disabled by the poisoning.

"That's a solid lead," LA agreed. "What I've heard of Grym is positive. He's a good cop."

"I agree."

"But I think it's a mistake not to connect the hobgoblin to what's happening with the youth magic," she said. "Where there's youth magic, there are generally goblins. And where there are goblins..."

"There are hobgoblins." She was absolutely right. I hadn't put it all together in quite that way. "You're a genius."

"Nope. Just far enough away from it all to see the forest for the trees. Find that hobgoblin, Naida. If you can make him talk, he'll probably shed a lot of light on things for you."

I'd make him talk all right. Even if I had to make him sweat brownie frosting for a month to do it.

14

GRYMLY DETERMINED

Grym asked me to pick him up at home for our trip to the cosmetics factory. That was a red flag right off the bat. He'd never asked me to drive. And I'd never seen his home before.

But he'd sounded like his normal self when we'd spoken on the phone, so that was good. Well, maybe a little more growly than usual. Like he was made of rock.

Wait...

I pulled up in front of a lilac, yellow, and pale pink Victorian home which had been turned into apartments. Despite being used for rentals, the beautiful architecture seemed to have been well-maintained, with fresh paint on the siding and trim, a nicely landscaped yard, and a roof that was, if not new, at least clear of debris and undamaged. There was even a guardian perched on its highest peak. No wonder Grym liked the place. They had a gargoyle on the roof.

The gargoyle shifted sideways as I pulled up under the shade of a huge oak tree.

Oh, yeah, Grym *was* the gargoyle. It seemed he'd taken Lea's advice to heart. He was still wearing his rock suit.

Grym dropped to a flat part of the roof and jumped, arms outstretched as he landed on his big, blocky feet and jogged toward my car. He stopped to grab a bundle of something from beneath the tree.

I could see why he'd asked me to park underneath the tree. Between the overarching branches, the thick trunk, and the heavy shade, he'd be hard to see for the rest of the neighborhood. His only area of vulnerability was the people inside the house.

Grym tugged my car door open and threw the bundle onto the floor, sliding inside. His knees were jammed up to his chest, and his head had to rest on them even with the seat as far back as it would go. He fixed a hostile, dark-caramel gaze on me and I grimaced.

"Sorry, this car wasn't made for gargoyles."

"This car is ridiculous," he growled out. "Why don't you have a real car?"

I took offense at that. I loved my beetle bug. "This *is* a real car. Besides, I get really good gas mileage."

"I guess it's better than walking. But not much."

He shifted slightly, smacking his head on the ceiling and putting a large dent in the fabric and foam.

"Hey!"

"Sorry." Grym tried to make himself more comfortable, apparently failing as his hostile gaze skimmed my way again. "Where's the power chord?"

"Huh?"

"For the car. Certainly, this thing doesn't use real gas."

"Har," I told the snarky gargoyle. "I wanted to ask you, Franny Clauss and Mrs. Foxladle stopped into the store yesterday. They told me Celia Pepper had boxes of creams and lotions to sell in her spare room. Did you find anything like that when you searched the place?"

"No. Only what was in the bathroom. The killer must have taken them out."

"That's strange."

I got the feeling he wanted to nod but restrained himself. He tried to scrub a rocky hand over his face and got it wedged, deepening the head dent he'd already made. I growled a little before I could stop myself.

"Maybe I should just run alongside," he said, looking miserable.

Yeah, that would go over well with the human population. "Or you could shift back to human."

He tried to shake his head, but it wouldn't move more than a centimeter. He sighed. "Your friend was right. This has limited the damage considerably. I don't want to change back until I have to." He gave me a crooked smile since half of his face was wedged into his knees. "Besides, I don't think you'd enjoy the results of that transformation in your car."

I grimaced. "Why? Do you leak fluid or something?"

His rocky brows lifted, waggling slightly.

"Oh," I said. "Oh!" Flinging a hand between us, I shook my head. "No, you're good the way you are. Just make sure you get out before you shift. I prefer that all skid marks remain outside the car."

His chuckle sounded like rocks sliding down a hillside. It made me smile.

I backed my little bug up and turned it, heading toward the street.

The shocks groaned under Grym's excess weight. I was pretty sure the tires on my side were barely touching the ground.

I needed to remember not to turn too quickly. My car might topple over like a turtle and not be able to get back up.

H*ebe Industries* was located about ten miles outside of Enchanted, in the center of a large industrial park with two other huge metal and stone buildings, amid a spiderweb of winding asphalt that seemed to feed more grass than businesses.

"Looks like there's room to grow here," I told Grym as I drove toward the largest building.

"I did some research on this place," he told me. "It's named after the Greek goddess of youth."

"No surprise there," I said.

"Right. But what might surprise you is that the company bought out the two other existing buildings in this complex and has managed to stop any more from being built."

My eyebrows climbed skyward. "Seriously? That would take an extraordinary amount of money."

"It would. So whoever owns Hebe Industries is either doing very well with their products, or they've got some pretty impressive backers and they're not just making wrinkle cream."

"How much money can you make on cosmetics?" I asked as I stopped in the road, eyeing the glass and stone front of the place and the parking lot filled with unimpressive cars.

"I'm guessing a lot." Grym pointed toward a copse of trees at the side of the road. "I'm going to jump out and go change."

"Change, huh?" I chuckled.

He rolled his pretty caramel eyes. "Wait here. I want us to arrive together."

Cold fingers danced up my spine. "You think we're being watched?"

He eased his bulk out of the car, somehow managing not to bend the frame of my car door. One big hand snaked back inside and grabbed his bundle of clothes. "Not yet. But there are cameras in those light poles. If there's something besides cosmetics going on inside that building, they're going to have pretty staunch security."

I skimmed a gaze over the building as Grym did his thing. Hebe Industries looked perfectly normal. Nothing about the place screamed of dastardly deeds and cold intent. But that meant nothing. Unlike in the movies, evil didn't send waves of warning out around it. It was generally just the opposite, in fact.

Evil generally kept a very low profile.

I was so caught up in my dark thoughts that I jumped when Grym wrenched the door open again. I pulled air into my lungs and turned as he slipped into the seat, examining him carefully. He looked about five years younger than what I guessed was probably his real age of about thirty-two or three. His skin was smooth, his eyes clear, and his sun-kissed brown hair was a bit on the shaggy side as it always was.

"You look better."

He nodded. "Let's get this done fast though. I could feel that stuff start attacking me as soon as I shifted."

Nodding, I started toward the lot, worry clawing

at my lungs. Grym wouldn't be able to do his job in his gargoyle state. He wouldn't be able to do something as simple as going to the grocery store for milk and cereal. I felt the weight of time settling on my shoulders even more than before. I was glad we'd found a way to slow down his descent toward destruction.

But that hadn't fixed anything. It had only given us a temporary band-aid to staunch the hemorrhage.

At some point, the bleeding would still prove fatal.

We parked and I walked alongside Grym with a heavy heart. He noticed my silence, sending me questioning glances that all but compelled me to tell him what I was thinking.

I managed to resist telling him that I was considering another trip to Madeline Quilleran's lair. I was ready to throw myself at her mercy...promise her anything she wanted...to have her fix what the evil youth magic had done.

Problem was, Grym was only one infected person. The fact that he was my friend made it feel worse. But if I didn't find that artifact soon, there were going to be more dying people.

And most of them wouldn't have the luxury of friends who could help them figure out how to cure the poison.

Or the ability to shift away from the body that was infected, to give them time to find a cure.

The lobby of the big building was devoid of life. Unless you counted the fish swimming around in the base of the two-tiered concrete fountain that dominated the space. The falling water was a musical counterpoint to my dire thoughts. I felt myself starting to relax almost immediately under its influence.

The lobby was tropical, filled with large green plants and trees in enormous pots and fed by a glass ceiling that showed the bright blue sky and the wisps of fast-moving clouds overhead.

A moment after we arrived, I heard the clip-clop of heels on the floor. We looked up to find a well-dressed woman hurrying toward us, her hands aflutter.

"I'm so sorry! I was all the way in the back of the production floor when I heard the bell." She gave us a smile, her perfect lips painted a pretty color of coral that matched her fingernail polish. She tugged the short, stylish jacket of her suit down in front and shoved a hand into a thick halo of blonde hair. Taking a deep breath, she offered her hand first to me, and then Grym. "Kat Geras. It's so nice to meet you." She glanced at the massive metal and glass clock on the wall. "You're early."

I blinked. "Early?"

Her smile slipped a bit. "Yes. Aren't you with Maycee's Department Store?"

Grym stepped closer, his own smile set to dazzle. "I'm Grym and this is Naida," he said, declining to clarify whom exactly we were with. "It's nice to meet you, Kat."

"The pleasure's all mine. Are you ready for your tour?"

"Of course," Grym said, "Lead the way."

He and I shared a glance as she turned her back. His message was clear. We would let her assume we were the Maycee's people as long as we could get away with it. I was okay with that. We hadn't lied. Exactly. But she might be more forthcoming if she didn't know Grym was a cop.

As we entered the massive production area, Kat turned to us, her voice lifted to be heard over the grind, growl, and clang of the equipment filling the room. "I hope you found your way to us without any issues."

"Absolutely," I said, then shrugged as Grym gave me a look.

"I was wondering if we could meet the owner while we're here?" Grym asked loudly.

"Oh yes," She screamed back. "Daddy's looking forward to sitting down with you to discuss distribution into your many stores." She threw Grym a smile that had enough heat in it to melt my polyester underwear.

I fought the urge to tug on said undergarment to make sure it hadn't adhered to anything important.

"We're very interested in how the creams are made," Grym yelled.

She frowned. "Creams? I thought you were interested in our lotion line."

Grym didn't miss a beat. "We are! Of course. But I've been thinking, what good is offering the lotions without the creams."

His grin melted my bra. *Lizard sneakers*! At least I'd have a matched set.

Kat laughed brightly, the tinkling sound somehow rising above the din. "You are so right, Grym," she told him.

When she turned away, I put my finger in my mouth and mock-gagged.

Grym lifted his brows in censure, but his lips twitched with humor.

I sent out my seeking magic as we started across a city-sized room filled with metal and rubber conveyor belt contraptions. Nothing came back to me, though we were potentially surrounded by some of the same cream that conceivably had killed the book club and apartment manager.

Kat walked all the way to the end of the room, yelling information along the way and greeting the men and women managing the addition of cream to jars and lids to bottles.

Hostile gazes tracked us across the room, distrust like a sour aroma filling the air.

The tour was interesting. The process of production was simple enough. Once the jars and bottles were sterilized and dried, they were sent along a steadily moving conveyor belt to a spot where labels were applied and then several perfectly spaced jars were filled at once with glossy white cream from funnels that hung from a large metal storage compartment. Before lids were added to the jars, white-coated attendants randomly selected jars of cream and performed a series of quick tests. Apparently, the contents of the jars passed the tests because no alarms ever sounded.

"What are they testing for?" Grym asked loudly.

"A variety of things," Kat answered. "Mostly acidity and purity." Her attractive face was smooth, her expression calm. She showed no signs at all of having doubts about their pretty product. After a moment, she pointed a well-manicured finger toward the end of the line. "Come on, I'll give you a sample to take home." She winked at me and I grinned, pleased that I wouldn't have to steal a sample as I'd planned. "I would love that," I told her.

The woman overseeing the boxing up of the final product at the end of the line fixed a dark, hostile gaze on me when Kat plucked a jar from her box, handing it to me. The woman's square face was mottled and pocked, her dark eyes deep-set. She looked down a slightly hooked nose at Grym and me. Her thin lips compressed with displeasure.

I gave her a smile as I accepted the jar. "Thank you." The woman's gaze narrowed, but she gave me a tiny nod.

Kat pointed toward a door on the far side. "The lotions are through there."

Fifteen minutes later, we exited the production area and entered the offices, which were located at the back of the huge building. My ears rang in the sudden silence and my pockets bulged with samples. Kat was a generous thing. Though, if she believed we were representatives from one of the countries largest department store chains, she could certainly afford to be generous.

"That was a great tour, Kat," Grym told her with a ligament-melting smile. "It's strange, though, I've lived in Enchanted all my life, and I didn't recognize a single person working in there. Do you bring your employees in from somewhere else?"

I knew what he was getting at, of course. I could only assume she didn't. I'd recognized the dark, deep-set gazes and square faces of a goblin in humanoid form. The ruddy, pocked skin was a dead giveaway.

Her smile tightened. Her gaze shifted briefly away. "We do, actually. Our employees are trained in Greece, where Daddy came from. We bring them here and give them jobs and a sense of family." Her smile softened again. "Their loyalty to this company is absolute."

Was there a hidden message in her words? Was she warning us of something? I just couldn't tell, but the idea of going up against an entire organization filled with goblins was daunting. I hadn't counted them as we walked through the production areas, but I figured there had to be close to a hundred goblins working at Hebe.

Too many to battle without creating a stir that would be frowned upon by the PTB and the Universe.

Unbidden, the judgy face of Rogers from the SDM flashed through my mind. The last thing I wanted to do was give him and the organization another reason to judge me unfit.

"Well," she said happily. "Shall we go talk to Daddy now?"

"That would be great," Grym said.

I gave him wide-eyes. We needed to talk to the salesman who worked with Celia Pepper. I couldn't help feeling as if our cover would be blown at any moment. After all, the real Maycee's representatives would probably be arriving soon.

He ignored me. But a beat later, as we approached a glass-walled offices, Grym stopped and placed a hand on Kat's arm. "You know what? I need to make a stop in the little boy's room. Do you mind?"

Little boy's room?

Kat nodded. "Of course, Daddy actually wasn't expecting us just yet anyway." She pointed down a short hallway. "It's down there. When you're done, just come through that door there and we'll get you in to see him."

"Perfect." He took her hand, holding it in both of his as he smiled warmly. "Thanks so much."

Flushing with pleasure, Kat melted into a puddle of goo right at his feet. I began to see how the Detective was so successful at his job. He could be very charming when he wanted to be.

Too bad he'd never bothered to use that charm on me.

As soon as she turned away, striding quickly toward the office, Grym jerked my hand and we headed for the hallway.

I threw a look at the man standing behind the floor-to-ceiling office window. He was diminutive and bent, his black hair painted heavily with gray. He looked at me through eyes that were glazed with age, his expression so filled with speculation it made my stomach twist.

"Come on," Grym urged. "I think I saw our guy."

I followed Grym into the hallway, but he didn't head toward the door clearly marked, *Gentlemen*. Instead, he hurried toward the open door to a room that emitted a stale fish smell that made my nose twitch. "Ew."

Grym slid me a look. "Goblins love fish." He grinned as I shook my head.

The man standing inside the small room was pouring himself a cup of coffee from a pot on the counter at the back of the room. The front area was mostly taken up by a round table of some kind of light-colored wood.

I skimmed my gaze over the microwave on the counter, the refrigerator, and the baskets filled with snacks alongside the coffee pot.

The man turned as we came through the door, his expression surprised. "Oh. Hello. Are you looking for Kat?"

He was pretty much just as I'd pictured him. The salesman was even younger than I expected, making a possible relationship with Celia Pepper even more suspect. If I had to guess, he was probably no older than early thirties.

Morial a.k.a. "Motoroil" Lipski, I assumed. Our salesman boyfriend. Grym had gotten his name from the company website when we'd agreed to visit the plant.

"No. We're looking for you," Grym said, reaching to close the door behind him. "I'm Detective Grym and this is Naida Griffith. My uh...civilian consultant."

The man's gaze altered from pleasantly surprised to startled when Grym turned the lock on the door. "Look, I..."

Grym lifted his hands, palms out. "Mr. Lipski, we don't want any trouble. I just need to ask you some questions about Celia Pepper."

The man frowned. "Celia? What about her. Is she okay?"

He seemed very convincing, but I knew a true criminal would be able to manufacture that kind of concern. "She's very sick," I said, praying Grym would go along with me. "She said you might have some idea why. Something to do with a cream...?"

He blinked. "The Fountain of Youth?" He paled. "Oh no, I told Kat that wasn't ready for prime time."

My eyes threatened to widen but I stopped them. "Really? What's wrong with it?"

He leaned back against the counter, forgetting the coffee cooling in his hand. "The tests we ran on the early formulas gave people a terrible rash on their..." He turned bright red, his hands creating a circle on the air below his waist. "Let's just say it was on a bad spot."

"Like diaper rash?" I asked, really working hard not to look at Grym. I could hear the detective growling softly. "That sounds really painful."

Lipski nodded. "I understand it is. I'm really sorry Celia is suffering. Kat promised me that side effect had been eradicated."

"Has it?" I asked, turning to stare at Grym. I couldn't help it, my lips were twitching.

He growled again, teeth showing, and poor

Morial Lipski took a step back. "Is there something wrong?"

"Yeah," Grym said, dragging his warning gaze from mine. I coughed over a chuckle. "Is this problem potentially fatal?"

Lipski's brown gaze turned bulgy. "Fatal? Oh my goodness...no." Tears filled his gaze. "Please tell me Celia's all right."

"She's far from all right," Grym told the man. "She's dead. Along with four other women who used the cream with her. And I believe the cream was directly responsible. We need to find out why and how, Mr. Lipski. But more importantly, we need to find out *who*. Right now, you're the only *who* we know about." Grym took a step closer, his body rigid. "Did you deliberately kill those women, Mr. Lipski?"

I thought Lipski might pass out. "No! I'd never. Celia was a friend." Tears slid from his bulgy eyes, his hands lifting to cover his mouth. "Oh, this is terrible. I'm going to tell Kat to stop production right away."

As much as I wanted that to happen, I recognized that he'd be in danger if he did that. If he truly *was* innocent, we couldn't let him risk ending up like those women. "You can't do that," I said, feeling Grym's stare as I stepped forward, going with my gut.

My instincts were telling me Lipski wasn't our killer. He didn't have the nerve for it. "If you do that she'll be forewarned. We need to find proof first. Can you do something to keep any more of the cream from being delivered?"

He thought about it for a moment and then nodded. "But you think Kat did this?"

I certainly wanted to think that. I didn't like her very much. She seemed too... What? Appealing to Grym? Nah, that couldn't be it.

"We don't know," Grym answered for me. "But we need your help, Mr. Lipski. We need to catch the person responsible for those women's deaths. Will you help us?"

He thought about it for half a beat and then nodded, sniffling. "Yes. I'll do whatever I can, Detective Grym. You have my word."

Grym rubbed a hand over his face, which I noticed had a sheen of sweat on it. "I'll want a list of all the stores that currently have this cream in stock," he told the salesman. "Can you get that for me?"

Lipski hesitated a beat and then nodded. "Kat and Mr. Geras will be out of the office this afternoon. I'll see what I can find."

15

A BOUNTY OF PROBLEMS

Grym stumbled slightly as we headed out into the hallway, throwing up a hand to lean against the wall. I glanced his way and saw the ashen quality of his face and the lines around his mouth. The artifact was starting to gnaw away at him again. We needed to get him shifted back to his supernormal form.

"Call me with whatever you find out?" Grym asked, handing Lipski the card he dug out of his pocket.

Lipski nodded.

"Anything else you think of...or if you see anything suspicious," Grym told the man. "I'd appreciate your insights."

Lipski's head snapped up as we came out onto the production floor. "There's Kat. She doesn't look happy."

I shoved Lipski's arm. "Go. We don't want her to see you with us."

As Lipski hurried away, I grabbed Grym's arm. His shirt was damp with sweat. "Let's go," I jerked him toward an exit straight across from where we stood. It was fifteen feet away. If we hurried, we might be able to get out ahead of Kat.

Lipski was right. The woman's previously upbeat expression was gone, obliterated under a pink face and eyes that flashed with rage. Behind her, two people in dark suits, a man and a woman, hurried to keep up with her long, quick strides.

The *real* Maycee's representatives, I presumed.

I hurried after Grym, who stumbled toward the door, leaning heavily on the sill of the main office windows.

Movement behind the glass caught my attention, and I looked up into the face of the owner, sucking in a surprised gasp to see him only inches away. Suddenly the thin glass barrier didn't seem nearly enough. I could feel his power pulsing against my skin through the window.

His eyes were dark gray, ancient and fierce. His face was heavily lined, the creases giving him a strange power that belied the years implied by his slight frame and bent shoulders. He wore his heavily grayed black hair slightly longer than fashion, and his lips were all but hidden beneath a thick mustache that drooped from the ends of his mouth.

His gaze when it fell on me was fierce.

With an effort, I jerked my attention away and scrambled after Grym. He shoved the door open and all but fell outside. I scooted quickly out behind him, ignoring the strident sound of Kat, screeching for us to stop.

Fortunately, we'd come out of the building close to where I'd parked my car. We'd parked on the outside edge of the lot so we could make a quick exit if necessary.

Thank the goddess, because as it turned out it was necessary.

The heat of a late morning sun beat down on us as Grym stumbled toward my car. I wrapped my arm around his waist and tried to help, but he weighed about a thousand pounds and it was like trying to guide a boulder across a steep slope. He kept veering away from me, and I was helpless to correct his trajectory.

Finally, I grabbed his arm. "Stop!"

A door slammed behind us. Panic made it hard to breathe. Kat was coming after us.

But when I looked up, it wasn't Kat I saw. It was the man with the fierce eyes and sad face.

He was standing a few feet from the door, staring at us, his small hands crossed before him. He had to be twenty yards away, but I could feel the bite of his power against my skin. Grym sagged downward. I couldn't stop him. He was too heavy and he had gravity on his side. He hit the side of a pickup truck and slid to the hot asphalt with a groan.

He needed to shift and fast, or he wasn't going to survive.

"Go ahead and shift," I told him. "Nobody can see you down there. I'll bring the car around."

He nodded and magic rippled on the air around him. I didn't wait to see if he managed the change. I took off running toward my car, praying Mr. Geras didn't follow.

Turning to see if he was still there, I breathed deeply under a surge of relief. The spot where he'd been standing was empty. There was no sign of him between me and the building.

He must have gone back inside.

Slowing my strides, I turned toward my car. Then jerked to a stop with a yelp.

Mr. Geras was standing a few feet away. Between me and my car.

I stared at him, unsure what to do. Power beat against me, compressing my chest until it started to hurt. My lungs stopped taking in air and needles prickled over my skin. I took a step back and then realized I didn't want to show him my weaker inclinations. Not yet, anyway. If he tried to use some of that terrifying power on me, I fully planned to run like the pansy butt coward I was.

The drooping mass of his mustache twitched

and the ends lifted slightly. I realized he was smiling. "Hello, Keeper."

I blinked. He knew what I was. Okay. I wished I knew what he was. "Mr. Geras."

The eyes narrowed on me but the smile, such as it was, remained.

"Why are you in my place of business?"

I had a decision to make. Did I come clean and ruin our chances of sneaking up on him if he was behind the deaths? Or did I try to keep my cards close? It seemed unlikely, given the amount of power he was sweating into the air, that I could lie to him about anything. Or catch him unawares. So I pulled as much air into my lungs as their clamped state would allow, and forced myself to step closer.

The fierce gaze widened slightly. I'd surprised him a little. It was good to know that was possible.

I hoped it was worth the embarrassing pit stains I was already creating on my blouse. "I think you know why we're here, Mr. Geras. Why don't you tell us what's going on?"

"Going on?"

I briefly considered the stupidity of egging him on, but figured it was my best chance to find out what he was about. And I was hoping his knowledge of my role in the magical power structure might save me.

Hey, I've always been a bit naïve. It's one of my more endearing qualities.

"Please don't play dumb, sir. My partner needs to get out of the sun (and his human skin) and we have five dead women to find justice for. Your magic anti-aging cream seems to be at the center of everything. I'd appreciate you being honest with me. But if you're not, we're going to find out what you're hiding anyway."

The mustaches assumed new depths of droopiness. "I'm not hiding anything, young woman. It's impertinent of you to accuse me of such a thing."

A brisk breeze filled with the scent of ozone blew past, tugging my long brown strands into the air and whipping them against my cheeks.

I looked up into the previously bright blue sky and saw a fierce wall of charcoal gray hovering overhead, lightning threading through the thick bank of clouds.

My gaze slid from the storm that had come up too fast, to the man standing in front of me with his small feet tucked tidily together and his undersized hands clasped in front of him. His old-fashioned suit was perfectly unwrinkled, and when the first drops of rain started to fall with an excess of energy upon my face and arms, the drops never touched him. "What are you?"

The question was through my lips and dancing on the air before I could stop it.

It elicited an answering smile on Mr. Geras's small, wizened face. "I'm the earth, the sun, and the sky. I'm time before it was measured and thought before it was realized."

Skunk's knickers! That wasn't helpful at all.

"Yeah but..."

Fortunately, Grym's heavy footsteps saved me from making a complete fool of myself. He came up behind me, still looking like death served on a shiny platter. He gripped my arm as rain pelted him on the face and turned his dark hair to glossy strings. "We're done here."

I let him urge me toward the car because I didn't want to be there anymore. But he stopped before he slipped into my vehicle and looked back.

Watching us, Geras stood with his hands clasped and his person completely dry.

Hail started to smack against my car. I yelped as it bit into my exposed flesh and dove inside.

"These people, humans, aren't your possessions. They aren't to be manipulated or used to further your products or your agenda," Grym told the other man. "You won't get away with hurting them."

Geras's reply was to smile, the mustache lifting high on his cheeks. "Clearly, you've never been in Sales," he said. And then he turned away and started toward the building.

In the blink of an eye, the rain stopped and the sun came back out, leaving only a distant rumble of thunder behind. Like a warning from the goddess.

"What was he?" I asked Grym, who was once again doubled over in my passenger seat, looking miserable.

He rolled his eyes in my direction, unable to move his wedged head. "If that was Mr. Geras, I'm guessing he's either the god of aging or he has a god as a sponsor. His power was off the charts."

"Geras?" I asked, my college classes in Greek Mythology coming back to me. "He and the goddess Hebe were tight," I said.

"Yep. Makes sense. Hopefully, they aren't in this together. It sure looks like they are."

I grimaced. "Awesome sauce. Do you think he killed those women?"

Grym's head moved a fraction of an inch, ripping the fabric in the ceiling of my car.

"Verbal answers only, please. My car can't take any more head-shaking attempts." I rubbed the little car's dashboard soothingly.

He sighed. "I don't believe in coincidences. I think it's too much of a coincidence that Celia Pepper was dealing in youth creams and then she dies the way she did. I also think it stretches credulity that the company that makes the youth cream is called Hebe Industries and it's owned by a man who calls himself Geras."

I'd been thinking the same thing. "So the only

question is, which of them is sending the poisoned artifact out into the world to kill people? Or is the entire company involved?"

"Technically, that's two questions," Grym told me.

I favored him with my version of Sebille's patented "You're an idiot" stare.

He grinned. Or at least, I think he grinned. Half of his mouth was smashed against one rocky knee.

I pulled into the alley next to Croakies and drove around back, hitting the button for the oversized garage door and driving through into the artifact library. I didn't generally park inside the library, but we needed to keep Grym's current guise under wraps.

Sebille hurried over and glared at Grym as he wrenched himself from my poor car.

"What's wrong?" I asked my assistant, feeling as if I'd rather run upstairs and hide than hear what she had to say. Lately, it seemed that if I didn't get bad news I got no news at all.

"We need to feed that frog large doses of something that'll make him sleep."

I frowned. "Why do you want Mr. Slimy to sleep?"

"Because I'm assuming he wouldn't talk while he was sleeping." She rubbed a hand over her eyes and sighed. "I truly cannot take another moment of his constant blathering. I'm going to hide in my room and drink tea." To my everlasting shock, she took off toward the back of the library, shrinking to bug size as she rounded the shelves and buzzing away.

I really needed to find time to ask her where she'd relocated. It seemed it was somewhere inside the artifact library. Hopefully, it wasn't somewhere dangerous or toxic.

I shook off that concern, not because I didn't care, but because there was only so much room in my head for crisis situations and I was full up.

In fact, I was overflowing.

Speaking of... I glanced at Grym. "You don't know anything about magic traps, do you?"

"No. What about them?"

"I apparently need one to catch a hobgoblin."

He narrowed his gaze at me. "What hobgoblin?"

Just then, Sebille buzzed back around the shelf. "I forgot to tell you, those furry hellions are back. Lea just came and took Hex home a few minutes ago."

"Thank the goddess," I murmured, closing my eyes in relief. My eyes snapped open to ask where they'd been, but Sebille was already gone.

"Naida? What hobgoblin?"

Firefly lightbulbs! He didn't know about *that* crisis. He'd been at home having a life and death crisis of his own when we discovered we were infested.

I sighed, leaning wearily against my car. "Rustin found hobgoblin dust in the bookstore after

Cinderella's wand cleaned the place to within an inch of its life. Literally."

He thought about that for a moment. "You know it had to come from..."

"Hebe Industries," I said, nodding. "LA helped me put that together. We're thinking maybe it's here to distract us from the artifact thing." I fell silent, frowning in thought.

"Who's LA?" Grym asked after a moment.

"My friend from Illusion City. A human familiar."

"I've heard of them. The human Familiars pretty much run Illusion City don't they?"

I nodded. "LA's wired in with all the magic users in this area. I wonder what she knows about Hebe Industries."

"It might be worth checking out." Grym rubbed a blocky hand over his face and took a step back. I looked up just in time to see him fall against a metal support column that creaked loudly under his weight.

I hurried over and looked into his eyes. They were red-rimmed and looked feverish. When I felt his rock-like flesh, I couldn't discern a fever, but I didn't know what a gargoyle's normal temperature was supposed to be. "Are you feeling worse?" I asked, chewing my lip with dread for his response.

He slid down the pole, dropping to his butt with

a "rocks hitting the floor" sound. "I just need to rest a bit."

"Why don't you go upstairs..."

He shook his head, closing his eyes and leaning his head back against the pole. "I'm fine here. I'll crush your furniture."

His eyes didn't open again. I reached out to give him comfort but changed my mind, pulling my hand back. I resisted the intimacy of that touch. Besides, I didn't even know if touch was comforting to a man who was made of rocks.

His big form quaked violently. Dread spread in my belly, causing it to twist with fear. The artifact had started to overwhelm even the special protection of being in his gargoyle form.

This was not good. "I'll just go up and get you a pillow and a blanket then."

I ran up the stairs, trying to think who I could call to help him. Madeline Quilleran's name stayed in the forefront of my mind. She'd had the embryo sample for several hours. Maybe she'd made some progress figuring out how to reverse the artifact poisoning.

As soon as I made Grym more comfortable, I was going to contact her. If she wouldn't come to us, I'd somehow get Grym to her.

A determined gray blur shot out of my apartment as I headed for the door. Mr. Wicked blasted past me and barreled down the steps with half a bagel hanging out of his mouth.

I opened my mouth to yell at him for stealing the leftovers from my rushed breakfast, but he was already out of sight.

I shook my head and continued on my way. I'd deal with Wicked's new bad habit later. After I got the other seven problems I was dealing with solved.

16

A DEARTH OF SOLUTIONS

I tucked Grym in as best I could and left him sprawled across the hard floor to check on Croakies. The store looked a lot better than it had the night before. All the books seemed to have been salvaged, and the carpet had never looked so clean.

I fixed myself a cup of tea, grimacing as I took a sip of the bitter brew. Where was Sebille and her tea-talents when I needed them?

A familiar green squish hopped up onto the tea counter and blinked at me.

After I recovered from the shock, I greeted the frog. "Hey, Mr. Slimy. How's it going?"

I'm glad you asked. I was wondering if you could tell me where your furry gray friend has gone? I've been looking for him all day, but he seems to have disappeared.

The complexity of the question shocked me a

bit. It seemed like Slimy's magic-infused brain might be gaining steam. "I just passed him on the stairs. He was hurrying somewhere with half a bagel."

Slimy blinked a few times, his throat expanding and contracting. Then he said, *Stairs?*

Okay, so much for the gaining steam thing.

I shook my head and grabbed my cell. LA didn't answer her phone, so I left a message for her to return my call and disconnected.

...hanging around with that little guy.

Slimy had clearly gone on talking while I left my message, but I'd only caught the tail end of it. I fixed my attention more firmly on the fat squish. "What did you say?"

He blinked at me a moment to let me know I was being annoying and then repeated what he'd said while I wasn't paying attention. *I said, Wicked walked through here with that little guy before, but he didn't stop to answer my questions about what he was doing. Nobody wants to answer my questions. I have so many questions. It's like this whole gigantic world has opened up and I don't recognize any of it...*

I held up a hand to stop him, starting to understand Sebille's frog fatigue. "I'll answer *one* of your questions. Then I'd like you to answer one of mine."

He thought about it for a heartbeat and then said, *Agreed.*

"Okay, shoot," I told him.

Shoot? As in propel bullets toward your physical body? Or as in point a camera at you and click?

I closed my eyes for calm. Apparently, with Slimy, we would have to ride the Literal Train to its final destination. "I meant, ask me your question."

Oh. Very well. Why is the sky blue?

Buzzard panties! How in the goddess's bunny-eared slippers would I know that? I thought about it for a moment and then said, "The Universe paints it once a century. I think the Trompe-l'œil clouds are a nice touch, don't you?"

Blink. Blink. Blink. *Yes, they're very nice. They look so real.*

I nodded my agreement. "Now it's my turn. Tell me about the little guy. Where did he come from?"

I don't know where he came from. He walked through that door over there by the small bookshelf. He looked around for a minute, saw me, and then hurried back through the door.

"He came from the artifact library? You're sure?"

If that's what's behind that door over there then yes.

I didn't like the sound of that. Not at all. "What did this little guy look like?"

Little, the frog told me with no apparent sarcasm.

"And?" I encouraged, trying hard not to reach out and pop him on the snout with a fingertip.

And what? He was small, bossy, and had a smudge of something above his lips.

I closed my eyes. A mustache might look like a

smudge of something to a frog who didn't understand the new world he'd been thrown into. Please
goddess he's not referring to Geras.

I opened my eyes. "Where did he go after he left
the bookstore?"

The frog gave a happy little hop. *Uh, uh, uh. You
said one question. That's three. I gave you one bonus
question, but I'm afraid I have to cut you off at two.*

I wondered if popping him on the snout would
do serious damage to the frog. I didn't want to hurt
him. Not really. I just wanted to bend him to my
will.

And take out my frustrations.

Okay, probably not a good idea to thump his
snout. I had a LOT of frustrations. I'd likely send
him sailing across the room. Sigh... "Okay, ask me
one more question. Make if fast."

All right. This one is really fast. Why is there air?

Goddess take the wheel.

Closing my eyes and counting to ten, I clenched
my hands together to keep from flicking him across
the room.

S ometime later...the duration of which felt
like days but was probably only hours...we
were sitting on the floor next to one of the
bookshelves and Sebille was helping me sort a new

delivery of books when Slimy hopped through the dividing door accompanied by Wicked.

"The prodigal son returns," Sebille said, looking disgusted. "What's he been up to lately?"

Wicked rubbed against my leg, purring, and I pulled him into my lap. "I'm guessing he and Hex have been searching for the hobgoblin."

She nodded. "At least nothing more has happened in the shop."

"Knock wood," I said. I handed her a new copy of *Advanced spells for Sour Stomach and Gastric Distress*, and she shoved it into the right spot on the shelf. I pointed to the thin volume on her lap. "You forgot one."

She looked down at the book on specialty tea blends for magical cures, shaking her head. "I'm buying this one. It has a lot of great information in it."

"You don't need to buy it, Sebille. Just read it and we'll put it on the borrow shelves. I've got a second copy on order anyway."

She frowned, finally nodding. "You sure you don't mind?"

I laughed. "I'm pretty sure I've already benefitted from a few of those spells. I'm all about you widening your repertoire of magical tea cures."

Sebille tucked a thick strand of bright red hair behind a pointed ear. "Thanks."

We worked in silence for a few more minutes,

the mundane task soothing my frazzled nerves. I'd placed calls with LA, Theo and Madeline, the last one through the mirror, and nobody had been available. Lea had promised she'd bring some herbal potions over that might help Grym, but I really needed to talk to the giant and get his trap. Sebille was right, things had quieted back down, but I couldn't help feeling as if it was the calm before the storm.

The front doorbell jingled. I looked up to see Franny Clauss coming into the store. She grinned widely when she spotted us on the floor. "What are you two doing down there?"

"Hi, Ms. Clauss." I shoved to my feet. "Just putting some new stock away. How are you today?"

Her gaze slid around the shop. "I'm well. Sad of course. But it's been therapeutic for Glenny and me to plan the girls' funerals." A shadow passed over her attractive face. I noticed the new lines around her eyes and mouth. Losing her friends had been hard on her. I reached out and squeezed her hand. "I'm so sorry for your loss."

She nodded, her eyes glistening with tears. "Thank you, dear. I actually came in to give you this." She handed me a small card with impeccably tidy handwriting covering it. "Those are the dates and times for the services. I thought you might want to come."

"Of course. Thank you for this. It was very kind

of you to come all the way over here. You could have called."

"I know. But I needed to get out of the house for a bit." She looked at the bookshelves, her gaze filled with longing. "Glenny doesn't want to talk about anything but funerals." She sighed. "She just seems consumed by guilt for not being there that night. As if her being there would have helped those poor women." Franny shook her head. "I just want life to get back to some semblance of normal."

I thought I understood her need to return to life before sorrow. Back to tea with friends and hours sitting in a comfy chair reading books from favorite authors. Which reminded me. I held up a finger. "Wait right here. I have something for you."

I hurried over to the sales counter and reached underneath it, grabbing the two books I'd rubber-banded together earlier on a whim. They were part of a new shipment of mysteries, and I happened to know the author was a particular favorite of Mrs. Foxladle's and Franny's. "These came in last night." I handed them to her and she took them like they were made of glass. Her gaze devoured the titles and then rose to mine, filled with wonder. "These just released today. How'd you get them so fast?"

I winked. "I have friends in high places." I actually had one friend, a Doppelganger spirit who worked for a publisher in New York and got me advance copies of the hottest new releases. "I thought it might give you both some relief from all the other stuff."

She sniffled, scrubbing the back of her hand under her eyes to catch the tears and gave me a one-armed hug. "That's so sweet of you, dear. Thank you."

She glanced around one last time, bent down to scratch Wicked's ears, and cooed at Mr. Slimy, who was a small green pile of corpulence and bulgy eyes near my cat. When she left, Franny was hugging her books to her chest as if they were the richest treasure.

My cell rang as the door swung shut behind Franny. I looked down and saw with excitement that it was Theo. "I'm so glad you called!" I told him.

"Hello, Naida. It's nice to speak to you too. How's Sebille?"

My gaze narrowed as I looked toward Sebille, still sitting cross-legged on the floor near the shelves. She was taking time during the lull in the work to look through her new book. Wicked was batting at the end of the string belt on her relatively sedate black dress. Though, when he jumped on her red and purple striped sock with the end of the string between his jaws, she grabbed at it and tugged, engaging a game of tug and chase that only made her more exasperated.

I hurried toward the door that divided Croakies from the artifact library, covering one ear to mute

Sebille's outraged shrieks. "She's great. Look, Theo, I have a problem. Do you by any chance have a magic trap in the shop?"

Theopolis Gargantu owned Enchanted's only pawnshop, named Enchanted Collateral. Like most giants, he loved to collect stuff. All kinds of stuff. Running a pawn shop was a great way to feed that love of junk.

"I actually do have a trap. Do you mind my asking why you need one?"

"I don't mind at all. Apparently, Croakies has become infested by a hobgoblin."

A heartfelt gasp came through the phone line. "Nasty creatures. They create all kinds of havoc. You need to get rid of it fast, Naida Keeper."

"That's the plan. Would you mind if I borrowed your magic trap, Theo? I'd owe you one."

"Not at all, Naida. Not at all. I'll be there in about an hour. I only have to find the thing. It's in my office somewhere. I just don't know exactly where."

With some intimate knowledge of what Theo's office-slash-home looked like, I grimaced. I figured if he showed up in a couple of hours, I'd be lucky.

Giants' homes were living artifacts, which, like the giants themselves, loved clutter and thrived on change. Even if Theo had seen the trap within the last hour, chances of it being anywhere near the spot where he'd seen it were minimal.

I thanked him and disconnected.

Movement near the dividing door brought my head around as Rustin eased into view. His gaze was intense, his translucent expression dire. "Naida, if you want to keep that 'goyle around, you'd probably better do something fast."

I shoved my phone into my pocket, hurrying toward Rustin. "What do you mean? What's wrong?"

He floated ahead of me into the artifact library. "I've been keeping an eye on him. Madeline's orders. A minute ago, he suddenly sat bolt upright, his eyes rolling back in his head, and his whole body started to tremble so hard I swear it shook the walls."

"Oh no! Grym!"

I dropped to my knees on the hard floor, my hands stretched toward the unconscious man. He'd shifted back to his human skin. He was so pale he looked like he was already dead. Froth covered his lips and blood flecked his chin. "He's coughing up blood," I said, anxiety making it hard to breathe. "Sebille!" I screamed, realizing as I did that I sounded unhinged. Panic had twisted icy fingers around my heart and was squeezing hard.

Sebille's red shoes clacked against the concrete a moment later.

I looked at Rustin. "Go! Find your aunt. I called her a couple of hours ago and she's not calling back."

He inclined his chin and disappeared. I prayed the tether between him and Slimy was long enough for him to reach Madeline.

Sebille ran over as I felt for Grym's pulse. I realized he wasn't breathing. "No, Grym!"

"What happened?" she asked, shouldering me aside.

"I don't know. It sounds like he had some kind of seizure."

Sebille placed her palms above Grym's chest. Green light bathed his skin, making him look even more sickly.

A moment later he twitched and his eyes flew open as he sucked in a gasp.

"Grym?" I said, moving around to his other side and clasping his ice-cold hand. "You stopped breathing."

He looked up at me, licking his dry lips, but before he could speak, his eyes rolled closed again.

"Sebille?"

"It's okay, Naida," she said, her tone cool. "He's just sleeping this time." She sat back on her heels, staring at him. "I wonder if it would help to put him into a natural healing cycle."

"What's that?" I asked, willing to consider anything.

"For lack of a better way to describe it, we basically bury him with a select collection of healing herbs. He'd have to stay that way for at least twenty-four hours."

I thought about her suggestion, my hand smoothing over Grym's strong arm as I struggled with the concept of burying him alive. "What are the chances that will heal him?"

"Heal?" She frowned. "We just don't know enough about the magic that poisoned him. I could be more certain if we did. But at the very least I think we can put him in stasis until we come up with a cure."

A cool moisture bathed my back. I turned to find Rustin hovering there. "Did you reach her?"

He shook his head. "No. And I'm getting worried. There are no signs that anybody's been in the house for a while."

"Maude?"

He shook his head. "Not even Maude."

Nausea blossomed through me. What in the names of all the goddess's cats did that mean? Then I had a thought. "Could she have gone to the Universe again?" Madeline had gone into the Universe with me recently to help me find the Power That Be who'd set a poisonous artifact loose on humans in my dimension. I found out later she'd been pursuing her own agenda when I'd thought she was helping me. A fact which didn't surprise me, knowing Madeline Quilleran as I did.

"I suppose it's possible," Rustin said, frowning. "If so, she didn't tell me she was going, which would be strange."

He was right. She most likely would have told Rustin. But knowing Madeline, it wasn't out of the realm of possibility for her not to have communicated her plans, even to him. "Okay, Plan B." I tugged my phone out as the front door to Croakies jangled. Lea's voice rang out.

"In the library!" I called back.

A moment later she hurried in, her pretty round face flushed. She carried a vial of something in one hand and wiped tangled blonde curls from her eyes with the other.

"He needs to take this..." she said, hurrying over to crouch beside Grym. "Help me get it down his throat."

"Wait, what is that? How did you know?"

"Lift his head, Naida!"

I was unused to my sweet-natured friend barking orders at me. I complied, but the urgency of her attitude made my pulse spike.

Lea managed to get most of the liquid down Grym's throat. It was a thick, muddy-looking mess that smelled like rotting vegetation. I grimaced as I caught a whiff of it.

She nodded as the last drop trickled into his mouth.

I gently lowered his head.

Lea stood and looked at Sebille. "Sindra has the plot prepared. We need to get him into it ASAP."

Sweat broke out on my brow. I swallowed hard. "He weighs a ton. How are we going to move him?" I asked.

"You don't have Aladdin's flying carpet here, do you?" Lea asked, giving me a weary smile.

I shook my head. "I did, but the PTB ordered it moved to another dimension." Something about fleas and magical transference. I hadn't asked a lot of questions at the time. I'd been busy trying to learn how to keep traveling artifacts from...well...traveling.

"We can move him," Sebille said, standing and hurrying toward the mirror.

"We?" I asked.

She touched the mirror with her fingertip, a thin stream of green light entering the glass and spreading across the surface. The magic hit the edges of the mirror and receded again, leaving a view of Lea's greenhouse behind as it went.

A fairy in the austere costume of Queen Sindra's guard buzzed into view. "What is it, Princess Sebille?"

Sebille's freckled face puckered with displeasure but she didn't yell at him for calling her Princess. It was one of her pet peeves since she wanted nothing to do with royalty or the ways of her people.

"Tell the Queen we need escort service for a heavy load. And make it quick. This is a life or death matter."

The guard doubled over in a low bow and buzzed quickly away. Sebille headed toward the back of the library, sending a bright jolt of magic toward the garage-sized door as she moved. Light flared around her and she disappeared from view with a soft pop, reappearing in her Sprite form. The size of a large dragonfly, she buzzed to meet the small army of Fae surging toward the door.

"This way," she told them, before hurrying back to Grym.

Lea and I stepped back as the Fae dropped to surround Grym in a buzzing outline. A soft green glow appeared underneath him. As the light grew, Grym's form started to lift off the ground. Once he was well above the floor, Sebille gave a soft whistle and the fairies shot toward the door, impossibly fast, disappearing outside.

I looked at Lea. "Well, that worked."

She smiled sadly. "Let's go. There's still work to be done."

Wicked followed me through the big door. I threw a bolt of magic at it to close and ward the entrance against unauthorized access.

My cat bounced along with me, batting at grasshoppers as we cut the distance between the back of Croakies and Lea's enormous greenhouse.

As we entered, I spotted the aura of the fairies' magic at the back of the big structure. By the time we reached them, they'd already lowered Grym into a deep hole they'd dug into the rich, black earth and lined with thick, shiny leaves.

The earthy scent of the dirt mingled with the

sweet smell of broken leaves as he sank into the prepared spot.

I looked at Lea, chewing my bottom lip with worry. "What if he wakes up while he's under there?"

She shook her head. "He won't. The elixir I gave him will keep him in stasis while the plants and earth heal him."

"How will he breathe?"

"How do any of us breathe? We take in what the plants give off. He'll be part of the same ecosystem, just in a more intimate way."

It made a twisted kind of sense and I trusted Lea. She was an Earth witch. If anyone would know this stuff, it would be her.

The Fae buzzed away from Grym and Sebille popped back to her full size. "He's ready," she told Lea.

My friend inclined her head. She reached down and broke several leaves from a nearby plant, folding them in half and pushing them carefully into Grym's mouth.

"What are those?" I asked.

"A magically enhanced type of Aloe Vera. The leaves will provide all the oxygen he needs until we pull him out of stasis."

When she was done, she stepped back and nodded toward the fairies. They surged forward, covering his entire form like a swarm of locusts. The sight made me hold my breath with worry. But as they streamed back, I was surprised to see that Grym was entirely covered in the black dirt.

Lea nodded her head. "That's it. He should be fine until I get the cure worked up."

I blinked. "Cure? You figured it out?"

Her smile was filled with pride and excitement. "I did. Well, Maddy and I did. It was a joint effort."

Maddy? "Then, why didn't we just give it to him?"

"I'm afraid it will take some time to create. There's one ingredient, in particular, that's going to be hard to get hold of."

"What is it? I can ask LA if they have any."

Lea sighed. "I doubt they will. It's a special flower called Devil's Crown. I guess it only blooms at night, in the desert, on the south-facing side of a mountain. Maddy's using her contacts to try to find it." Lea wrapped an arm around my shoulders. "We'll get it done, Naida. Now that we have a little time I'm confident we can save Grym."

I nodded, chewing my lip with worry. I really hoped she was right.

17

INTO THE BUBBLES YOU GO!

*B*y the time the bell jangled on the bookstore entrance, I'd almost forgotten about Theo's imminent arrival.

When I glanced up from my book order, I found myself looking into his wide, happy face below the top of the doorframe.

He ducked through the door, easing himself slightly sideways to fit his enormous bulk through the normal-sized entrance. "Hello, Naida Keeper!" His booming voice made Slimy jump against the glass wall of his tank, his black eyes bulging more than usual.

I came out from behind the counter and walked over to the giant, offering him my hand. "Thanks for coming, Theo."

He shoved my hand aside and wrapped me up in a hug that totally engulfed me. I was surrounded by heat and the sweet scent of cookies. Being around Theo always made me hungry. Giants loved sugar, especially in the form of baked goods, my own personal favorite, and he always smelled like carb heaven. "I'm so sorry to hear about your infestation, Keeper," he told me as he let me go.

"Thanks. Did you find the trap?"

"Yes. It took a while." Theo grinned.

Yeah, I'd noticed.

He patted the large, square pockets of his tan corduroy coat, a blast from the fashion past, and stuck his hand inside the right one, drawing out a purple plastic bottle with a white label and handing it to me. "This will take care of your little problem."

I looked down at the label, which depicted kids blowing iridescent orbs through a small wand. "Bubbles?"

He nodded, his brown gaze sparkling. "Delightful, huh?"

"You mean I could have just gone down to the Penny store and bought some bubbles to use as a magic trap?"

He blinked. "What? No. Of course not. That would be silly. I ordered this from the Universal Mass Online Retailer. UMOR for short. It's a huge online magic supply store. You can only reach it through the Dark Web."

I filed that away for later use. Unscrewing the

bottle, I sniffed the contents. It smelled fruity. Like grape juice. "How do we do this?"

"Have you purified with Sage?"

I nodded. "After you called." In between burying my friend alive and trying to run a business.

"And you have the brownies?"

"Brownies plural? LA said I'd need one."

The giant grinned widely. "The second one's for me. I'm famished."

Laughing, I went to retrieve the small box from our favorite bakery. "Fortunately for you, the Sprite went to get them and she always gets multiples. Hopefully, she left two..."

Theo extended his hand and took the greasy cardboard, grabbing one brownie from it and shoving the box inside his coat. "Perfect. Would you like me to do the honors?"

"Be my guest." I handed the bottle to him.

Theo extracted the wand and tapped it against the bottle a few times, shaking off the excess liquid. What was left created a glossy web that covered the entire circle at the end of the wand. He bent down and set the bottle on the ground, placing the brownie on top of it, and motioned me back. I watched, fascinated as Theo shuffled his feet a few inches farther away and leaned over the bottle, the wand held upright.

He turned to me. "Ready?"

I nodded, not sure what I was getting ready for,

but if it meant catching the little jerk who'd made a mess of my life lately, I was definitely game. "Ready."

Theo closed his eyes, murmured something I didn't catch, and then flung the wand into the air.

I watched it topple end over end for a beat and then stop, hanging in the air directly above the bottle. Theo took another step back and urged me to do the same.

Light shot from the bottle in a cylindrical burst that filled the matching circle on the wand and expanded outward, a glossy column that caught the various lights in the store and threw them back in a rainbow of colors. The brownie levitated above it, the delectable scent of chocolate filling the room.

The lights were pretty. The magic was quivery like bubbles. And the spell throbbed with latent energy, giving off a high-pitched range of sounds.

The bottle spun, faster and faster, as the wand rotated in the opposite direction at the same, impossible speed.

After a moment, they both stopped spinning with a shriek and went perfectly still. For the single beat of a heart, the magic waited, and then exploded outward in a wash of bubbles, covering everything in the center of the bookstore in a grape-scented gloss of cool magic.

I sputtered, scrubbed my hand over my face, and coughed as the tinge of sulfur in the magic caught at my dry throat and irritated the tender tissue there.

When I opened my eyes again, I blinked.

The bottle of bubbles was tipped over onto the rug, spilling a puddle of liquid onto my carpet. The wand still hung in the air, steady and unmoving. Between them, encased in a lustrous column of magical energy, stood a tiny creature with sharply pointed ears, large blue eyes, and a long nose shaped like a bent funnel over full pink lips.

He was already popping the last bite of brownie into his mouth as my gaze found him.

The hobgoblin blinked in surprise, its little head, no bigger than my fist, rotated from me to Theo and then back again.

"Is it trapped?" I asked Theo.

He nodded. "Yep."

"How do I release it?"

Theo's eyes went wide. "Release it? Why would you do that? Just have your Sprite blast it with magic and eradicate it." Theo's lips curled. "Nasty critter."

I didn't miss the judder of fear that slammed through the little creature at Theo's harsh words, or the way the cute little shock of light brown hair between its ears quivered along with its body. The hobgoblin was dressed in a small white smock, its wiry arms and legs sticking out of the garment. Its feet were bare, slightly oversized, and each big toe had a tuft of hair on it that matched the tuft between its ears. The hobgoblin's fingers were long, on tiny hands. They constantly clenched and unclenched while plucking nervously at the smock.

But it was the eyes that held me in thrall. They were beautiful, with long lashes, and they were filled with expression. Mostly fear and pleading.

In that moment I knew I could never hurt it. "Thanks for your help, Theo. I'll return the trap after..." I made a motion with my hands that I hoped he would assume meant I'd deal with the creature as he'd recommended.

"No worries, Naida Keeper. It's spent now. You can just order me a new one on UMOR."

"I'll do that."

I waited until he'd left to sit down on the ground in front of the hobgoblin. Mr. Wicked plodded silently into the room and rubbed against the bubble holding the little creature. I was shocked to see the critter's blue gaze soften as it looked at my cat.

"Have you two already met?"

I realized as I asked the question that they most certainly had. Wicked had no doubt been hanging out with the hobgoblin wherever it lived. Bringing it half-eaten bagels and goddess knew what else.

In fact, I was guessing it was his influence that had halted the pranks that had caused so much stress and work.

I looked into the creature's beautiful, terrified gaze. "I'm not going to hurt you."

It shuddered violently, clearly not believing me.

"I promise."

The hobgoblin tilted its head, the tiny hands reaching out to rest against the bubble holding it there.

"What's your name?"

The creature looked at Wicked.

My cat meowed softly, climbing onto my lap.

The hobgoblin sighed, a whisper of sound that made its bubble prison shiver. "I am Hobs."

Of course he was.

I smiled. "I'm Naida. And apparently, you've met Mr. Wicked."

The hobgoblin's lips curved upward in a slight smile. "He is my friend."

I hugged Wicked close, earning myself a lick on the nose and a smack on my cheek with a paw.

"Ribbit!" Mr. Slimy objected.

I nodded in his direction. "That's Slimy. He says hello."

I can speak for myself, young woman, Slimy said in a snotty voice. *I was just reminding you not to be rude about introducing me.*

I rolled my eyes. "Is there a reason you sound like my grandmother?"

The frog ignored me, speaking to the hobgoblin. *I'm happy to meet you, young man.*

Hobs turned around and gave Slimy a little bow. "Mr. Slimy, it is my pleasure."

Such nice manners. Maybe Theo was wrong about hobgoblins. "Hobs, can you tell me how you came to be here, at Croakies?"

The hobgoblin turned back to me, his spidery fingers twisting together with sudden nerves. "I'd rather not, Miss."

"You can call me Naida."

The blue eyes went wide. "Oh no, you shouldn't, Miss."

I frowned. "Shouldn't what?"

"I could never call you by your true name. Names have power. Never give that power away, Miss."

"But you gave me *your* name," I reasoned, frowning.

Hobs bowed his head. "I have no power, Miss."

Sadness filled my chest. "That isn't true."

He sighed, his chin resting against his chest. "But it is true, Miss."

I looked at Wicked. "How do we break the trap?"

Wicked stared back at me for so long, I started to think he hadn't understood me. But I couldn't be wrong about his intelligence. He'd proven to me over and over again that he was intuitive and skilled with magic. Alone, and in conjunction with my meager stores of energy. Just as he'd been bred to be.

There's meaning in releasing him, Naida. Slimy said. *Wicked wants you to be sure you understand that you're giving him freedom and a certain level of autonomy by letting Hobs out of the trap.*

I shoved irritation and not a little jealousy away. It wasn't fair that the frog could understand my cat and I couldn't. Maybe I wasn't trying hard enough. Maybe if I worked at it, I could open that channel of communication like I had with the frog.

But that was a problem for another day.

I nodded. "I understand what releasing him means, little man."

"Meow," Wicked put his paws on my chest and rubbed his head under my chin, purring loudly. Apparently, he approved of my decision.

Wicked jumped off my lap and ran toward the magic trap, poking it with his nose and sneezing. He walked around it a couple of times, tail snapping as he assessed the magic involved. Then he lifted a paw and unsheathed his claws, smacking it hard.

The glossy column of magic disappeared with a soft pop and a wisp of grape-scented air.

Hobs dropped to the floor, landing on his over-sized feet like a cat.

He slowly pushed to his feet, his blue eyes wide with uncertainty. "Miss?"

"You're free, Hobs. You don't work for me or anybody else."

The enormous eyes blinked slowly as he seemed to consider that. "But I've never been free, Miss. Where will I go? What will I do?"

Oops. I hadn't thought about that. "Um…"

Wicked rubbed against the little creature, nearly toppling him sideways with his exuberance.

Stumbling a couple of steps away, Hobs giggled, sounding like a happy toddler. I found my own smile forming.

"I'd be happy to give you a place to stay here at Croakies," I held up a finger as the hobgoblin's face lighted with pleasure. "With one very important caveat."

The light left his little face. I regretted his apparent misunderstanding. He clearly thought I was going to make him work for me or something equally restrictive.

"I only want your promise that you won't mess with the artifacts. We have some really dangerous ones in the shop and you could endanger all of us if you set the wrong one free."

Hobs nodded eagerly. "Yes, Miss. You have my word."

"Good," I said, offering him my hand. "It's a pleasure to have you here, Hobs. I look forward to getting to know you better."

He looked at my hand as if it were a nest of snakes. When his eyes lifted to mine, I gave him a slight nod. "It's okay. I want us to be friends."

"Friends, Miss?"

He spoke in a tone of awe and disbelief. "Friends. Like Wicked and Slimy. They're your friends. And…"

I slammed my lips together. I'd almost said Sebille would be his friend too, but there was no way to predict that. It would be best if she didn't know about our little deal for a while. Until I could prove to her that it would be okay. "And if you decide you want to leave, you're free to go."

The long-fingered hands plucked at the smock and Hobs' huge eyes turned glossy with unshed tears. "You're a goddess, Miss."

"Oh, heavens, no." I snorted out a laugh. "I believe everyone should have a chance to make their own decisions and create their own perfect life. That's all."

Hobs stepped forward and slowly, with great uncertainty, offered me his little hand. I took it, feeling the solemnity of the moment in the tightness of my chest. His skin was warm and soft and the backs of his fingers were covered with course hairs that matched the strands on his head. "If it suits, Miss, I'll be pleased to help where needed."

I thought about all the dusting I never had a chance to get to and nodded. "I appreciate that."

I shoved to my feet, glancing from Wicked to the frog. "Until I have time to tell Sebille about this new arrangement, mum's the word. Capish?"

"Meow," Wicked said in agreement.

Is that another question? Slimy asked coyly. *Because, if it is, I have a question of my own that I need an answer to.*

Holy Banshee tears. The frog was going to be the death of me.

"She was blonde, Miss."

I looked down at Hobs, frowning. "Excuse me?"

"The woman who brought me here. She was blonde and smelled like flowers. But she was really more like a prickle plant."

Kat! I knew it. "The woman from Hebe Industries?" I asked, just to make sure we were talking about the same prickly blonde woman.

Hobs's, forehead wrinkled. If he'd had eyebrows, it would have been a frown. "She has goblins." For just a beat, the little face darkened with anger. "Horrible creatures, goblins."

Well, that was good enough for me. I had my killer.

All that was left to do was figuring out how to capture her without Grym.

Which reminded me. We needed to heal Grym.

And we needed to force Kat to give me the artifact.

Then I needed to lock it safely away.

And finally, I needed to make sure there was no more tainted cream out in the world to poison more unsuspecting humans.

Sigh...

18

EUREKA!

I sent Wicked and Hobs off to play in the artifact library, after warning them to stay out of Sebille's way. Before Wicked would leave, he ran over and put his paws up on Slimy's enclosure.

I sighed. "Okay, but don't get the fat squish into trouble back there, you two."

I scooped Slimy out of the glass tank. His nasty tongue snapped out, barely missing my face. I jerked backward. "Argh! Ew!"

I don't appreciate being called fat, he told me with a blank, bug-eyed look. *It hurts my feelings.*

"Okay, sorry." I settled him next to Wicked. "I didn't know you *had* feelings."

Why wouldn't I have feelings? he groused as he hopped after the other two. *Besides, I've seen your backside when you bend over. It's a bit like the pot calling the kettle metal.*

"Well..." I jammed my hands on my hips, knowing he was right and even more irritated about it. "So that just happened."

Sebille clomped through the door, a large paper sack in her hand. "It's been a tough day. I needed tacos."

I felt my eyes glaze over at the delicious scent. "Please tell me you brought me one?"

She snorted. "As if."

My shoulders sagged and my lower lip tried to poke out. To my credit, I did bite down on it to keep myself from looking like a petulant five-year-old.

"I brought you three. You need to keep the cals rolling if you expect to maintain that door stopper you call a backside."

Zeeeeeppppp! "I can't believe you just said that."

She cackled meanly. "Have you met me?"

She had a point. But I was starting to get a complex.

Shoving pride aside, I accepted the three hard-shelled chicken tacos she pressed into my hand and sat down at the round table near the stacks. "I found out who's responsible for the cream. We just need to figure out how to trap and force her to give up the artifact." I took a big bite, sighing happily.

"Who is it?" Sebille tossed a short stack of napkins in my direction and sat down across from me.

"Kat Geras. Daughter of the owner to Hebe

Industries." *And possibly a genuine goddess*, I couldn't help adding inside my head.

Sebille swallowed. "Any idea what kind of artifact we're looking for?"

"No." I frowned. There *was* a way to find out what kinds of artifacts stole a person's youth, but Osvald had told me not to call him again. No, that wasn't exactly true. He'd told me not to open the *Hobgoblins and other Pesky Vermin* book. He hadn't said anything about opening another book of his. "It was a lot easier to do my job when I received orders for the artifacts I needed to round up."

"Yeah, what's going on with that, anyway? I thought Madeline Quilleran was working on finding out what's wrong with the system?"

I shrugged, stuffing the last bite of my second taco into my mouth and chewing thoughtfully. When I'd swallowed, I said, "She's been called away on PTB business. I have a feeling it might have something to do with that."

Sebille nodded. "At least she gave Lea what she needed before she left. I'm a little surprised she stooped to working with another witch."

"Yeah. Me too. It concerns me a little bit. Lea seems almost...smitten with Madeline. I still don't trust her, and I don't want Lea to get hurt."

We ate in silence for a moment before I glanced up. "Any word on how Grym's doing?"

"Nothing specific," Sebille responded. "Our healers are monitoring him, and his vital signs are strong. I think he's safe where he is until Lea can finish the cure."

"I'm worried somebody else will succumb to this cream," I told Sebille.

"Have there been any more attacks?"

"Not that I know of. Which is strange. It's almost like the killer preselected the book club and never planned to go beyond them." I shrugged. "It's something to think about."

A frigid touch of air wafted over my shoulder. I looked up to see a misty spot morph into a tall, handsome ghost witch. Rustin peered at us in disgust. "Do you two ever do anything other than eat?"

Sebille and I shared a look, shrugging. "Sometimes we sleep," I offered, grinning around my last bite of taco.

"You're just jealous," Sebille taunted him. "You wish you could eat tacos."

Rustin grimaced. "It would definitely be better than crickets and those other disgusting things you feed the frog. Can't you feed him a burger once in a while?"

Fighting a grin, I shook my head. "What can we help you with, witch?"

Rustin sighed. "I wanted to let you know that

Madeline just sent the last piece of the puzzle to Lea. We now have the cure for the youth artifact."

"Sweet Caroline!" I exclaimed, surging to my feet. "I'll go see her now."

L ea was staring down into a small jar filled with a green mash when I came through the door into her shop, *Herbal Remedies with Mystical Properties*. The sweet scent of fresh green herbs hit me as I came through the door. I inhaled deeply, pulling the soothing scents in and letting them perform their magic on me. I had a smile on my face as I headed for Lea. "Rustin just gave me the good news."

But the expression she turned my way wasn't a happy one. I felt hope crashing and reached out to grab hold of the counter, bracing for the news. "What's wrong?"

Lea shook her head. "I'm so sorry, Naida."

Stars burst before my eyes. I swallowed hard as I fought my instinct to cover my ears and run from the room rather than hear what my friend was about to tell me. "Wh..." The word caught in my throat. I cleared it and tried again. "What is it?"

"This won't work on Grym. I tested it against a sample I took from him before we put him into stasis."

"The cure doesn't work?"

She took a deep breath and let it out, long and slow. "It works. But not for him."

I frowned. "Explain."

"We created the cure with plant magic. Earth magic. But Grym's basic make-up isn't of the soil or the plant. It's..."

"Mineral..." I said, feeling hope crash around my feet. "He's aligned to rock, not plant."

Lea nodded. "It didn't occur to us that there would be a difference. But this cure had no effect at all on the youth magic in his system."

My legs gave out and I leaned heavily on the counter, my world wobbling as I felt my friend slipping away. "Can't it be adapted?"

"Maybe," she said. "Probably. But I'm not sure he has that much time."

I shook my head, desperate to deny the truth of what she was saying. "There has to be a way."

"I'll keep working on it, Naida. You know I will. But it will take time..." Her voice fell away as if she didn't have the will to finish the thought.

She didn't need to finish the sentence. I heard the words she didn't say in my mind.

Time we don't have.

Then I remembered what I'd learned. I looked up. "I know who created the youth magic. We just need to catch her and get the artifact."

"If you have the artifact, can you reverse this?"

I nodded with more certainty than I felt. I wasn't sure how the artifact we were looking for worked. But I would find a way. I didn't have a choice. Grym's life depended on it.

I shoved to my feet. "I need to gather the troops. We have to figure out how to lure this piece of troll dung in and capture her."

Lea nodded, reaching out to clasp my arm. "I wish I could help."

Cold realization hit me. Lea wouldn't be able to help. I couldn't draw her away from trying to find a cure for Grym. If we couldn't get the artifact and reverse its effects, her efforts might be the only thing that saved him.

I nodded. "I know you need to stay here and keep working. We'll figure this out."

But as I strode quickly from her shop, I couldn't help thinking that I was really up against a wall. I didn't have Lea. I didn't have Grym. I couldn't count on Madeline Quilleran to help.

And we were going up against a creature of enormous power.

How on earth were we going to win the battle we had to fight?

In the end, I was terrified that Grym wouldn't be the only one who lost his life.

"Sebille!" I slammed the door behind me and started pacing the carpet in front of it, thinking. I could ask Sindra for help. Her Fae army would be a formidable ally against Kat. I could ask Theo. He'd be good for brute strength. I wondered how I could find out about the other cops in Enchanted who were supernormal friendly? That would take a bit of thought. Of course, Grym would know. And Madeline...

I sighed. I kept crashing up against the same wall.

"Sebille!!!"

"Hold your panties!" my assistant growled as she slouched into the bookstore, her arms filled with books. "I heard you the first time you bellowed."

"What took you so long?" I asked, peering suspiciously at the three large volumes nestled in her bony arms. "What are you doing?"

She peered toward the stacks, holding a finger over her lips. "Mrs. F, are you finding what you're looking for?"

I felt my eyes go wide. I made an "oops" face and went in search of my favorite customer, finding her sitting in one of two upholstered chairs I'd placed in a small open space among the shelves. She sat with her head back and her eyes closed. For one terrifying moment, I thought she'd passed out. Or worse.

"Mrs. Foxladle?" I hurried over and touched her

arm, relieved to feel that it was pliant and warm. I gave her a little shake. "Mrs. Foxladle? Are you all right?"

Her eyes fluttered open and she blinked up at me as if she didn't know where she was for a beat. Then she smiled. "Oh my." She chuckled, sitting straighter in the chair.

I heard Sebille's heavy footfall behind me. "Would you like some tea, Mrs. F?"

The older woman smiled past me. "Yes, thank you, Sebille, dear. I'd love some tea."

When Sebille left to make the tea, Mrs. Foxladle patted me on the arm, chuckling. "Don't look so horrified dear. I might be old, but I'm not quite that old yet. I'm not going to wander in off the street and drop dead among all my friends." She waved her arms to indicate the shelves of books.

"Oh, I didn't..."

"Of course, you did, hon. It's okay. I'm sure I look like death warmed over. To tell you the truth, I'm just exhausted. I never realized how much work would be involved in planning all these funerals." Her voice broke on the last word. She took a shuddering breath. "I hope you don't mind. I just needed to get away from it all for a bit."

Sebille handed a steaming cup of tea around me.

"Don't be silly. You're welcome here any time. I mean that sincerely." I straightened, smiling down at her. "I'm sorry you're having to do all that planning. Didn't your friends have families who could help?"

She sipped her tea, a rosy flush infusing her crepey cheeks. "That's delicious, Sebille. Tea always tastes so much better when you make it, hon."

"Sebille is tea-talented," I told Mrs. Foxladle with a grin.

"She certainly is. If I didn't know better, I'd think she infused each cup with magic."

I gave Sebille a look. She waggled her brows at me, mouthing the word, "brandy" and making me choke back a laugh.

That would do it.

"In answer to your question, Naida, no. Celia's son is hiking a mountain somewhere and will be lucky to get back in time for the funeral. Nan's family is gone. Mei-ling's family lives in Thailand. They're much too poor to come, I'm afraid. And Bonnie's daughter apparently hasn't spoken to her for years. I'm not even sure how I'd find her to tell her about her death." She sighed, the lines between her eyes deepening. "I'm finding out that loneliness was probably what made my friends join the book club in the first place." She smiled sadly. "But I think in the end the books had become just as much their friends as we had."

"I'm so glad you ladies found each other."

She nodded, glancing up. "You know, Franny and

I are continuing the book club. We're looking for new members. Maybe you and that nice police detective would like to join?"

I smiled. "Maybe we would. I'll certainly ask him when I see him again. But whether we join or not, I'd be pleased if you held your meetings here at Croakies. And I can put a flyer out about the meetings if you'd like."

"That would be wonderful! I'll talk to Franny about it when I get home."

"Good. I'll just leave you to your rest then."

I headed back up to the front of the store and found Sebille perched on the tall stool behind the sales counter, perusing one of the books she'd brought from the back. I started toward her just as the dividing door between the library and the store opened. Mr. Wicked popped his furry head through and pushed to widen the crack.

I'd love to know how he managed to open that door by himself. Maybe I could post a camera nearby to catch him in the act.

My eyes went wide as Hobs bounded through after him, his pointy ears bouncing as he hopped like a frog. The hobgoblin grinned shyly at me, his cheeks pinkening.

I dropped a hand down by my hip and motioned with my fingers for him to return to the library, but to my horror, he got a mischievous look in his eyes and, in a flash of movement so fast my eyes couldn't follow, he cut the distance between the door and the first row of shelves and climbed to the top.

I glared up at him and he waved gaily, disappearing again so quickly I didn't see where he'd gone.

Something thumped to the floor a moment later, followed by a soft cry. I gritted my teeth, hoping Hobs wasn't up to mischief, and hurried back to where I'd left Mrs. Foxladle.

She was flipping through a paperback, her eyes alight and her smile wide. She looked up when I came around the end of the shelves. "I've been looking for this book for weeks. I can't believe you have a copy here," she told me, her cheeks pink again.

I looked up to where Hobs crouched atop the next row of shelves. He winked at me.

Shaking my head, I sliced a finger across my throat and pointed at him.

He flashed away again, leaving behind the faintest echo of laughter.

I hurried toward Sebille. "What are you looking for?"

She was on the last book of the three. The other two lay open beside her on the counter.

"Artifacts," she said softly. "So far, I've found these," She lay the third book down next to the other two and I pulled it close, looking at a picture of a garter. It was black with white lace sewn down the center and a small yellow flower adorning the top.

"I'm having trouble seeing any of the ladies wearing a garter to book club, let alone sharing one," I told Sebille.

"I agree," Sebille told me. "I think this one has a much better chance of being the right one."

It was a small porcelain figurine of a ballerina. The dancer had rosy cheeks and was wearing a soft pink tutu. The flat toes of her pink ballet slippers were attached to a dove-gray-colored base. The ballerina held a long-stemmed red rose in one hand, the glossy petals pressed against her tiny nose. "This one," I told Sebille. "Older ladies love to collect stuff like this."

"That's what I thought too," my assistant said. "This one's also a possibility, but I like the glass doll better."

I turned the last book around so I could examine the image. As I placed my hand on the page, the center bubbled, and a figure started to ooze upward out of the book.

Osvald's dark head spun around. His gaze found mine, widening in shock, before he pointed his nose toward the book and dove back down, disappearing into the page.

I looked at Sebille and she shrugged. "I didn't do anything to him. He did the same thing to me."

"You didn't do anything to him?" I asked, my gaze narrowing. "Why would you say that? I never asked if you had."

She pursed her lips, pretending to study the porcelain figurine.

"Sebille?" I asked again in a sterner tone.

She lost the battle against a grin. "I might have told him I was going to a book burning tonight and offered to make him nice and toasty around the edges if he didn't disappear himself."

I cleared my throat, looking down so she couldn't see my lips twitch. Finally, when I thought I had my grin under control, I looked back up. "Bad, Sebille. Very bad."

She snorted out a laugh, pointing to the second book. "It says here the figurine was Hebe's favorite of her collection of porcelain dancers. Apparently, it spins and plays elevator music."

"Elevator music? That's odd. Don't you mean classical music?"

"Classical music, elevator music, potato, pototo." She shrugged again. "It's the kind that could put you to sleep even with a giant slice of chocolate cake in your hand."

"I'd say it's a safe bet Kat still has the figurine in her possession, probably at the plant since she's using it there to create her creams." I had a sudden thought and smiled. Maybe we wouldn't have to face off with a powerful goddess after all. "We need to sneak inside that plant and search her office."

It was no surprise to me when Sebille's eyes lit up at the prospect. A little breaking and entering was right up Sebille's alley.

Emphasis on the breaking part.

19

B&E WITH SPRITELY GLEE

The parking lot was well-lit, even in the wee hours of the morning. Fortunately for me, I had a Sprite with anger issues and a propensity for breaking things on my side.

It took Sebille only a few minutes to buzz around and darken one side of the lot to cover our movement toward the back door Grym and I had used the last time we'd been there. It took her only thirty seconds to open the locks on the door, and it took me only five seconds to trip over the mat on the inside and fall flat on my face.

Sebille stepped over me, disdain dripping from her like melting ice, and I shoved to my feet with my pink face and skinned knees.

The illumination in the area consisted of low wattage lighting placed at just above floor level, clearly meant only to keep someone from falling in the dark on the way to the main office.

Or, at least that had been the idea. I'd always been good at overcoming best-laid plans. Think of me as a prodigy and then multiply that talent by two.

I carefully avoided Sebille's gaze and pushed past her, feeling the roll of her eyes like a force in the air.

May the force be with you. It was certainly with me.

"Where to?" she asked, clomping up behind me in her ill-fitting red shoes. Sebille had purchased the Wicked Witch of the West lookalike shoes on sale at a bargain shoe store and had insisted she couldn't live without them despite the fact that the only size they had was a size and a half bigger than Sebille's feet.

The office door was unlocked and I pushed on through, drifting past the exterior desk, which I assumed belonged to some kind of assistant or greeter, toward the two doors with rippled glass insets marked with the names of the owner and his daughter, one Katherine Geras.

I stopped at Kat's door and listened but didn't hear anything. "I think we're good to go," I stage whispered.

Sebille nodded, raising her brows. In the low illumination of the night lights, I could clearly make out the impatient expression on her lean, freckled face. Sebille wasn't built for stealth. She was more a "bustle in and bust 'em up" kind of gal.

But then, if things went south as they were wont to do when we followed Sebille's methods, she could always pick up wing and fly away, leaving me earthbound and magic-less to deal with the fallout.

Well, essentially magic-less anyway. I could make someone pee their pants in a heartbeat. Or frizz their hair to within an inch of its life. But that was pretty much the end of my magic juice unless that someone was an artifact. Then I could kick their artifact butt all over the place.

I slowly turned the knob and eased the door open. Kat's office smelled like Lilacs. Her desk was tidy to the point of looking like it had never been used.

Every item, from the dainty upholstered chairs to the glass and chrome desk, to the dense furry rug that dominated the center of the space, was tidy and perfectly arranged, as if she'd gotten a Master's degree in Feng Shui and a doctorate in OCD.

The office was pleasant and attractive, much better suited to a high-priced lawyer's space than the office of an employee of a cosmetics production company. But it was cold, calculated, and, like the desk, felt as if it had never been used.

It didn't take us long to search the place for the artifact. Kat Geras was not the type of person to collect stuff that would collect dust.

Sebille and I split up and took different halves of the room. When we met in the middle, our hands were empty.

"Maybe she took it home with her," Sebille offered, frowning.

"It's possible. We'll need to get her home address. We can break in there in the morning while she's here at work."

Frown disappearing at the idea of more B&E in her near future, Sebille nodded. "Let's go get ice cream."

"Okay, but not at the place with the sign that lures you in. That's an artifact, I'm sure of it."

She shrugged, opening the door to Kat's office and stepping into the outer office. "So what if it is? It's not hurting anybody."

"Says the woman whose backside is *not* being referred to as a door stopper," I responded.

Cackling at her own joke, Sebille took a step toward the exit and jolted to a stop. I slammed into her back. "Umph!"

Rubbing my nose, I stepped around her. "Warn a girl if you're gonna stop…" My words trailed off at the sight of two very large…men…for lack of a better word, standing between us and the door.

I swallowed a lump in my throat and tried a smile. "Is this the Ladies room?"

Sebille snorted and I pinched her arm.

"Ouch!"

"What were you two doing in the boss's office?" the larger of the two growled out.

"Um..." I'd never seen goblins up close and personal, but as I looked into their dark, leathery faces, fierce black eyes, and shark-like double rows of pointy teeth, I decided I could have gone a lifetime without the pleasure.

There was no hint of the human façade the men no doubt donned when working the assembly lines during the daytime.

"We had an appointment with her," Sebille said, slouching casually against the receptionist's desk and crossing her arms. "She stood us up."

The smaller of the two goblins, not really small at all, given that his friend was probably close to seven feet tall and he was only an inch or two shy of that, narrowed his wide, black gaze and pursed scabby looking lips. "She didn't tell us nothin' about no meetin'."

Sebille grunted, shaking her head. "That's horrible English. Didn't they teach you goons nothin'?"

The two stared at her, looking perplexed for a beat, and then decided to solve their problem with violence. I got the impression that wasn't a hard decision for them. They probably solved all their problems that way.

Growling loud enough to make my bladder

dance the pee pee dance, the goblins jumped, flying through the air with the greatest of ease.

When they landed, their fists came crashing down in the spot where we'd been, rattling the teacup and saucer sitting on the desk with the force of the hit.

Sebille buzzed away, leaving a cackle of glee in her wake, and I scrabbled behind the desk, my knee throbbing where it had hit the chair when I'd jumped out of the way.

It didn't take long for them to reset and move, one of them coming after me and one flailing around its head trying to smack a buzzing Sebille out of the air.

Footsteps pounded toward me, and the chair suddenly flew past, crashing into a potted plant in the corner.

Green energy flashed across the room as I leaped to my feet and grabbed the first thing I saw on the desk. Infusing my hands with keeper energy to give them speed, I grabbed the long metal object and a sheet of paper and screamed as I was hit with the force of a runaway train.

I crashed to the floor and grunted as the goblin landed half over me.

Panicking, I shoved the paper at its face and slammed the stapler against it, putting several staples through the paper as he screeched in rage.

While he fought to rip the paper away, I shimmied out from under him and headed for the door.

A big hand grabbed my hair and yanked me to a stop. I yelped in pain, trying to reach the doorknob but missing as he dragged me backward.

Green energy flared again. The goblin released my hair, screaming and clutching his eyes as he stumbled blindly around the room.

Sebille popped into full size next to me. "That was fun."

I glanced around. "Where's the other one?"

She jabbed a finger toward Kat's office. The goblin was sitting on the floor, leaning against the door, his chin resting on his chest.

"What did you do to them?"

"Nothing yet," she said with a grin. She lifted her hands and shot twin beams of green energy from them. "There. Give me your phone."

"My phone? Why?"

She wiggled her fingers until I handed it over with a sigh. "We need to get out of here. There might be more of them," I told her.

She took a picture of the goblin by the door and the one that had fallen next to the desk and then showed me the phone.

The two men were wearing tutus. Pink ones, and had large pink bows resting in the bald spots between their bat-like ears.

I snorted out a laugh. "Perfect."

"Not yet." Sebille pecked out some commands on my phone and, a moment later, I heard the sound of a message being delivered. She handed the phone back to me. "*Now* it's perfect."

We got out of there fast. I didn't ask her where she'd sent the pictures until we were in the car.

Her response was pure Sebille. "I'm tired of pussyfooting around. It's time to bring Kat to us."

Holy buzzard blisters! "You didn't!"

She lifted her finger and blew on it like a gunslinger clearing his weapon.

The shop was dark except for the Frog-shaped nightlights near the door and behind the sales counter.

"Tea?" Sebille headed for the tea stuff while I locked the door behind us.

"Yes! Please?" Weariness slid over me and my stomach growled hopefully. "I don't suppose you have any more of those tacos?"

Sebille handed me a steaming cup. It smelled like rosemary and something minty. "Sorry. I can make a run if you want."

"No, it's late. I have bagels and fruit upstairs. Would you like to join me?"

"Sure."

We started toward the stairs. I opened my mouth

to ask her where she'd moved her stuff, but Wicked flew down the stairs with a yowl and Hobs slid down the banister behind him, giggling maniacally as he hit the curved part at the bottom and flew through the air, smacking hard against the wall and sliding down, arms and legs splayed like a cartoon character.

He lay there twitching and I let out a terrified sound of concern. "Hobs!"

It didn't take me long to discover he was twitching with laughter. When I turned him over, tears were running down his face. He clutched his belly, his grin wide. "Again!" he suddenly yelled, launching to his oversized feet and flying back up the stairs.

I turned around and got caught on Sebille's glare. She stood with her arms crossed, and her bright red eyebrows arcing into her hairline. "Oh, yeah, about that..."

"You let it stay?"

"Um,"

"Ribbit!"

I looked up to find Slimy perched on the top step, looking stuck. "How in the world did you get up there?"

"Meow!" Wicked wound around my ankles, purring. At least he was happy to have a new playmate.

With a delighted shriek, Hobs flew down the

banister and splatted into the wall, cackling breathlessly.

Sebille rolled her eyes. "I can't believe you let it stay. Do you know how much damage it will do?"

Hobs shot past up the stairs again. A beat later, he flew down and hit the long arm of the law...a.k.a. Sebille...when she stuck her bony limb out to stop him before he launched.

"Umph!" he grunted, toppling backward off the banister and hitting the concrete floor with another grunt.

"Sebille!" I hurried around to do CPR, arriving just in time to see the hobgoblin leap to his feet and yell, "Again!"

I sighed, shaking my head. "I couldn't exterminate him, Sebille. And I couldn't just cast him out onto the street. He's just a kid, really. He has nobody. He had no place to go. I know I should have sent him on his way but...I just couldn't."

She stared at me for a minute and then slid a look toward the creature sliding down the banister. Hobs's eyes were bright with hope that she would knock him to the floor again.

Sebille happily complied.

I groaned as he hit the concrete even harder than before.

"Wait for it," Sebille said.

"Again!"

She grinned like a Cheshire cat as Hobs shot up

the stairs once more. I realized in a moment of horrifying clarity that Hobs was Sebille's perfect playmate. He was like the Wile E. Coyote to Sebille's Roadrunner or the Charlie Brown to her Lucy.

I grabbed Hobs before he could charge back upstairs. "That's enough fun." I carried him squirming and laughing up the stairs. "Can you grab Slimy?" I asked Sebille.

When I had all three of the trouble makers confined in my apartment, I got food out of the refrigerator and we fixed ourselves a hodge-podge of a meal.

After we'd eaten, I sat back, rubbing my full belly. "So, Sebille, tell me where you went? Where are you sleeping?"

She shrugged. "In the library."

I hadn't seen her stuff in the library, anywhere. I knew it was a big place, but not big enough to hide the multitudinous collection of furniture and stuff my assistant had. "Where in the library?"

She shrugged. "We need a plan to deal with Kat."

Yeah, we did. Especially since Sebille had thrown the gauntlet down in front of the powerful goddess. "Do you have any ideas?"

She shrugged. "Wait for her to come to Croakies and then kick her butt."

"Simple. Elegant. Monumentally stupid," I said.

"What do you suggest then?"

"We have a problem. Actually several of them.

We can't ask Madeline to help us because she's gone. We don't have Lea because she's fighting the clock trying to help Grym. And Grym...." I let that thought slide away, the ending too obvious to state.

"So, you and I will take care of her. I'm sure mother would send some of her guard if we need them."

"I don't think you understand how much power we're dealing with here. Her father saturates the air around himself with the stuff. Even if she isn't as powerful as he is...and I have no idea if she is...he's not going to let us play whack-a-goddess and just look the other way."

We'd basically be dealing with both of them.

"I repeat. What do you suggest?"

I sighed. I didn't have any idea how we were going to pull it off.

Hobs jumped up and stood on one of the empty chairs, his liquid gaze fixed longingly on the leftover fruit.

I shoved a thick wedge of apple his way.

Watching him eat, it occurred to me he might be able to tell us more about Kat. "Hobs, the lady who brought you here, did she have a lot of magic?"

His eyes went wide and his fingers stilled. "Yes, Miss. She hurt Hobs."

Sebille shifted uncomfortably in her chair. "You mean, like shoving you off a banister?"

Hobs grinned. "No, that was fun!"

Sebille grinned back. "It really was, wasn't it?"

I glared at Sebille before returning my attention to the hobgoblin. "Did you ever see a porcelain figurine at the lady's house? A ballerina?"

Hobs said the word *ballerina* softly under his breath as if trying it on for size. "What is that?"

Sebille went downstairs and brought up the book, showing Hobs the picture we'd found earlier. "Like this?"

Hobs nodded enthusiastically. "Yep. But it wasn't at her house, Miss. She carries it with her always. I like to listen to the pretty music and watch the lady dance."

I frowned. "The lady dances?"

"The pretty lady spins and spins."

I realized he was talking about the ballerina. Apparently, it played music. I looked at Sebille. "That must be how it spreads the magic?"

She nodded. "If she always carries it with her, how are we going to get the thing away from her."

Inspiration struck. I glanced at Sebille, excitement making me bounce in my chair. "I know how we can beat her!"

Sebille waited with raised eyebrows.

"The pavilion at the park. It amplifies magic. If we put all the magical energy we can gather under that pavilion, we might just be able to trap her."

Sebille thought about it for a moment and then

nodded. "Okay, that might work. But how do we get her there?"

"I can get the lady there," Hobs said, licking juice off his chin with a disturbingly long tongue.

"You can?" I asked the little creature. "Are you sure?"

He nodded enthusiastically. "I'm sure. If I can have some peach to take with me."

I shoved a slice of peach toward him. "If you can get the lady to the pavilion for us, you can have all the peaches you want, Hobs."

20

BACK TO THE MAGIC

*A*s before, the moon hung high and fat in the sky above the pavilion. The silvery glow bathed the grass around the structure, painting the tips of the leaves and creating a pretty pattern on the floorboards beneath our feet.

The usual sound of the crickets was accompanied by the insistent buzz of fairy wings as Queen Sindra's guards flew the perimeter, setting spotters who would let us know when Kat arrived.

I half expected the woman to just drive up and park in the lot, assuming her arrogance would give her a sense of invulnerability against us. Plus, if Hobs did his job, she wouldn't be expecting us to move against her, she'd be looking for victims for her youth-draining magic and she'd expect us to be unsuspecting dupes.

Thinking of Hobs, I frowned, my stomach churning with worry. I knew he was a wily little guy, and I'd given him instructions not to take unnecessary risks, but I couldn't shake the feeling that I'd sent a puppy into a den of wolves and it was making my heart pound a little too fast.

Or maybe that was just sheer terror of what we were about to do, which was on a slow drip through my chest.

I'd never gone up against a god-like entity before. I'd only ever been around one once. Geras's power had made it hard to breathe when I was standing several feet away from him. I couldn't imagine what he or his daughter would be capable of if threatened into an active fight.

Rustin floated over and offered me a phone. I slid my gaze over him as I took the phone from his hand. The power-enhancing energy of the pavilion had boosted the ghost witch's form, making him look almost fully corporeal. His handsome face was pinched with worry and I knew that was partly because we couldn't reach his aunt. And partly due to the news we'd received right before we'd left Croakies to come to the park.

Area 51 had called to tell us Margot Quilleran had somehow shaken off the four-dimensional glamour spell Lea had layered onto her and disappeared from the prison facility. The assistant to the warden hadn't been sure if she'd escaped or if trying to beat the glamour had killed her, turning her cock-roach form to dust on the floor of her cell. He'd told us that the iron box she'd been kept in was twisted and half-melted away, and he was afraid she'd gotten out.

I added that to the long list of things to worry about.

Shoving all worries of the Quilleran enforcer aside to be addressed later, I focused on my current problem. I had bigger buttocks to blister at the moment.

I looked down at the phone and saw Lea's name. "Hey! Did you find the cure?"

Lea sighed. "Not yet. I'm so sorry."

I felt bad for putting pressure on her. I knew she was working as hard and as fast as she could. "No, I'm sorry for pushing. It's just a little nerve-making here."

"I can only imagine. I called to tell you that Theo's on his way and he's bringing Birte with him."

That was great news. I had no idea how much good the giant could do, he was mostly brawn, with little magic of his own, but a fire-breathing dragon could definitely prove useful. "Thank the goddess," I breathed. "What about Madeline?"

"Sorry. I only spoke to her briefly and we talked about the cure. She didn't have much time and I figured that was priority. I did manage to ask her about defeating a goddess and she said, they get their power from legend."

Butterfly bunions! "What does that even mean?"

"I don't know. Maybe to defeat them you need to affect the legends somehow?"

And that was no help at all. Unless we could figure out a way to go back in time. I bit back a sigh, not wanting to make Lea feel worse than she already did. "Okay. Thanks for the good news about Theo and Birte."

"My pleasure. I'll get back to work."

As I disconnected, Sebille buzzed toward us, a soft green glow making her easy to see in the dark. I hoped she could extinguish the light when Kat got there. Otherwise, she'd be much too easy a target to hit.

"The Fae are in place," Sebille reported. "I just received a report that a car has entered the park."

I sucked in a deep breath, trying to calm my heart. Swiping my moist palms over my jeans, I peered up at the sky, looking for Birte. "Any time now, Theo," I murmured to myself.

I glanced at the picnic table behind me. Slimy and Wicked sat on the tabletop where I'd put them when we'd arrived.

Wicked was bathing a paw as if the world wasn't about to end and Slimy was eating, a limp insect leg dangling from between his lips.

Ugh!

A wave of cold fear bloomed in my belly as the harsh reality of my situation hit me. It was me and Sebille, a ghost witch, a dozen Fae soldiers, a frog and a cat against massive power the likes of which I'd probably never see again.

What could possibly go wrong?

I heard tires on the gravel road and turned to Rustin. "Let's do this."

He nodded, bending down to put the finishing touches on the trapping sigil he'd drawn across the floor of the pavilion.

A light-colored sedan eased into view around the last bend in the park road and I narrowed my gaze on it, feeling as if I'd seen it before. As it drove into the lot, the moonlight painted the windshield, briefly illuminating the pretty strawberry blonde in the passenger seat and the dark-haired, square-jawed man who was driving.

I grinned, clapping my hands as I ran to greet my friends.

LA laughed as I threw myself at her, giving her a heartfelt hug. "You came!" I'd called her earlier, hoping I could entice her into my nightmare, but she hadn't answered her phone, so I'd left her a message and prayed she'd get it in time.

"Sorry I missed your call. Deg and I have been up to our necks in troll politics at Familiar, Inc."

The organization her grandmother had started served as ground zero for the governing elite and magical politics in Illusion City. The downside of LA being involved was that, as one of the governing council's newest members, she spent way more time than she'd like dealing with inter-house squabbles and tedious entreaties by the magical members.

I gave Deg a little wave as he climbed out of the car. As always, I was struck by the dark good looks of the powerful witch.

He smiled my way. "Hey, Naida."

"Thanks for coming, Deg. I owe you big time!"

He shook his head. "Believe it or not, I'm relieved to be here. Anything to get out of political Hades."

The back door opened, and a tall woman with silky black hair that fell to her shoulders climbed out.

"Naida, this is our friend, Mandy. She's a goddess with potions."

Mandy gave me a cool, quiet greeting as three gray cats with yellow to orange eyes jumped from the car.

I squealed happily. Wicked yowled his delight and jumped down from the table, running to greet his littermates. All we were missing was Hex. And I was pretty sure Lea wished she and Hex could be there with us.

"You'll have to stop by Lea's shop and let Hex see the kids before you go back. She'll be so disappointed she missed them."

LA nodded. "We'd planned on it. Now tell me

what's going on." She looped her arm through mine. We started back toward the pavilion. The kittens took off across the grass, tackling each other and rolling around biting and playing, long tails snapping the air with happy exuberance.

I quickly filled Deg, Mandy, and LA in on our nemesis and the limited resistance I'd been able to cobble together so far.

LA grinned when I told her about the dragon and giant who were coming. "Sweet!"

"Hopefully Brock and the dragon won't bump into each other up there," Mandy said in a throaty voice filled with arrogance.

When my eyes widened in surprise, LA nodded. "We brought the demon. But he didn't want to ride in the car. He claims he's allergic to magical cats."

I laughed. "Knowing Brock, he just wanted to scope out the area before the fun started."

"I'm sure that's part of it," Deg said, his dark silver gaze sliding over the sky. Despite the bright, nearly-full moon overhead, clouds had begun to gather above us, occasionally obscuring the silvery light we needed to generate the power-enhancing effects of the pavilion.

The worries that had plagued me since setting off on our nearly impossible journey returned in full force as a particularly dense bank of clouds swam over the moon.

As the clouds skidded on their way, the moonlight once again painting the clearing, my heart stopped beating for a moment. A dark form with huge wings overlaid the moon for a beat, the sight too reminiscent of the Quilleran enforcer in her predator shape.

"There's Brock now," Deg said, pointing.

I pulled air into my clenched lungs and closed my eyes in relief. I really needed to find my chi or I was going to have a stroke right on the spot.

The enormous creature flew straight toward us until he reached a height of about thirty feet and then he used his wings to slow his descent and lowered his feet so that, by the time his shoes hit the grass, he just took a step and continued walking toward us. It was the most beautiful landing I'd ever seen.

A demon Brock might be, but he wasn't evil. At least not in the classic sense. LA had told me enough times how much he liked to tease and torture her for me to know that he was demonic like a bratty younger brother might be.

However, I had exactly zero sisterly feelings toward the ten feet tall demon with clawed fingers and thirty-foot-wide, sawtooth-edged wings. He was as terrifying as he was beautiful. Brock reached for my hand as he approached, folding his wings tidily along his back. "Naida," he kissed the back of my hand and I heard Sebille sigh next to me.

"Ribbit!"

I looked down to find that Slimy had come to greet our newcomers. I scooped him up as the kittens ran over to check him out, unsure whether they would be as kind to him as Wicked had been.

Since he flies, maybe this one could tell me why there's air since you've failed so miserably at it, Slimy groused.

LA sucked in a surprised gasp. "He's talking now?"

"Yeah, unfortunately. Apparently, he's ingested some residual magic from having Rustin on board."

LA and Deg had aided me in our failed attempt to separate Rustin from his frog bus. Despite not having been successful, or maybe because of it, they'd stayed interested in Rustin's progress.

Speaking of the ghost witch. Rustin came over and greeted my friends with a nod. "Thank you for coming to help."

Ignoring his stiff behavior, Deg reached out and slapped him on the back. "We can't afford to let this artifact go unchecked. It might make its way to Illusion City."

Rustin nodded.

"I'm going to do recon," Brock said, before jumping down off the platform and taking a running leap into the air. I watched his formidable wings drive him smoothly into the sky, his muscles bulging attractively with his efforts. I must have sighed because LA cleared her throat.

"Ah, the lure of the bad boy. It's almost irre-sistible," she said.

I flushed with embarrassment. "Who me?"

LA laughed. "So what's the plan?"

I explained to her about the pavilion's special magic. "As far as we can tell, Kat's got god-like powers. We're seriously out of our league here. I'll take any advice you can give me on how to take this woman down."

Deg looked at Rustin's trapping spell. "With the cats here, I could give you some ideas for how to strengthen that."

Rustin and Deg walked over to the collection of symbols and sigils, talking and pointing.

Mandy set a black bag on the picnic table. "I've got some potions that should help." She pulled out a large jar filled with a swirling green cloud. "This will redirect any energy she flings toward us right back at her. She can't destroy herself with her own energy, but she can definitely slow herself down."

"I love that idea."

Mandy pulled out two more jars, they looked like they were empty. "These obfuscation spells will make us blend into the background. I thought Deg and Brock could use them. Maybe they can sneak up on her if we keep her distracted enough."

I nodded. "Great."

Mandy held her fingers up and showed me a small capsule. "This is for you. If this woman is as powerful as you believe she is, your normal keeper magics might not work with her. She'll be able to offset them to keep you from retrieving the artifact. This will enhance your power twenty-fold."

I took the capsule with a grin. "Any chance you could make me up about a hundred of these?"

Mandy didn't laugh. "No."

I blinked rapidly, staring into the witch's humorless, caramel gaze.

Awkward Aardvark!

"Alrighty then." I popped the capsule into my mouth and swallowed, feeling it burn its way down my throat and sizzle in my belly.

After a moment, I felt a surge of power that brought heat to my cheeks.

"Be careful with that. You're not used to the kind of power you have right now. Don't hurt yourself with it," Mandy said with just the tiniest bit of condescension.

I managed a nod at the surly witch and then watched her move over to the edge of the platform to begin pouring the contents of the green jar, which was less gaseous than I'd first thought and more granular.

"Ignore Mandy," LA told me, her blue-green gaze sparking with good humor. "She's kind of a sourpuss, but she's got a kind heart."

"I'll take your word on that." I glanced worriedly up at the sky as another bank of clouds moved in. "I hope the moonlight doesn't let us down at the moment of truth."

LA frowned. "The pavilion depends on the moonlight?"

"That's my understanding."

The dark deepened until I couldn't see into the yard anymore. A cold, musty breeze slipped past, bringing gooseflesh up along my arms.

Something tugged in my center, like a warning, and I felt LA stiffen beside me.

"Deg," I heard her whisper.

His response came from nearer than I'd expected and I jumped. Somewhere out in the hazy dark, there was movement.

"We need light," LA told her witch.

"I'm on it."

Another wave of moist, musty air slipped past. Wicked wound around my ankles, his soft warmth jolting me from my rigid fear.

Who's the woman? Slimy asked.

My chest tightened. "What woman?" I asked softly.

The one standing in the grass. She's got our friend Hobs with her.

The frog could see through the deep, unnatural dark.

"Is Hobs all right?" I asked him in the softest whisper I could.

He doesn't seem happy, but he doesn't look hurt.

A slow clapping sound cut through the thick, oozing black air. A faint light bloomed about fifteen yards from the pavilion, illuminating a slender form wearing a long, black dress. "I'm impressed, Naida Keeper," the woman said, her voice distorted by the fog swirling around her form. My gaze slid upward, looking for the source of the light that almost illuminated her but not quite. I thought I could make out a blonde halo of hair on her head, but I couldn't see her features through the mist. "I didn't think you'd have the gumption to take me on."

I stared at her for a moment, stalling for time and, hopefully, a return of the moonlight. Then I forced my stiff lips to smile. "I just want the figurine. Give me that and you can go on your way."

"I'm afraid I can't do that, dear. I'm not quite done with it."

"What exactly are you trying to do? Why did you kill those women? They didn't do anything to you."

"An unfortunate outcome, I'll agree. Would you believe me if I told you I never intended to kill them? They were merely guinea pigs. If things had worked out I'd have made them supremely happy. They'd have been young again." Despite her words, there was no regret for their deaths in her voice. Only disappointment that it hadn't bought her the desired goal. "I'm having a bit of trouble getting the formula just right. But I'm very close now. After tonight I believe I'll have what I need."

I didn't like the sound of that. Clearly, she'd come to the clearing with the idea of harvesting us for her deadly experiment. "Formula for what? Hasn't Hebe Industries already cornered the market on anti-aging creams? Are you trying to make more money? Because, if that's what you're doing, you've been going about it all wrong. Killing your target market isn't exactly a winning strategy."

Her laughter hit the dense, wet air and died before it fully bloomed. "Hebe Industries is a joke. Geras enjoys being ancient and wizened. He has no idea what he's done to me."

Something about what she said set off warning bells, but I couldn't quite put my finger on what it was. "What has Mr. Geras done to you?"

"Isn't it obvious, dear?" She lifted her arms and the haze surrounding her swept away.

I gasped.

She raised her fingertips, running them over her wrinkled cheeks and touching the dark circles under her eyes. "He's taken away the thing that makes me what I am. He's using my very essence to create in others what he's taken from me."

Sebille was suddenly standing beside me. "Isn't that..."

I nodded, shocked beyond words. She'd been right under our noses the whole time.

"I'm a little dense," I finally choked out. "Tell me

exactly what he's taken from you...shall I call you Franny? Or do you have another name? Like Hebe?"

"Since the beginning of time, I've been Hebe, the Goddess of Youth," she said, through gritted teeth. "Until that wrinkled gremlin of a man stole my youth magic from me."

21

OOPSIES!

*F*ranny Clauss was Hebe, the Goddess of Youth? I was gobsmacked, shocked beyond words. I would have never guessed. But seeing her there, it made perfect sense. She'd hidden in plain sight among the people she planned to use to regain her youth.

I wondered if there were others we didn't know about, who'd given their lives to her experiment. I found it hard to believe her rampage of thoughtless killing had started and ended in Enchanted.

"So, are we to assume you're draining these poor people to regain your youth?"

"I'm only trying to take back what's mine."

"And is it their fault you lost it? Why don't you try to get Geras to return your youth instead of killing innocent people?"

She shrugged. "He has proven immovable on the

subject. I'll have to take my pleasure from ruining his company once I've gotten my youth back." She smiled. "It will be a shame when the world finds out what his creams have done."

I frowned. "You can't make it public knowledge, and you know it. The Société of Dire Magic will be all over you like caterpillar panties. They'll take you down." *Then maybe they'll leave me alone*, I thought unhappily.

Her smile was mean. "They can try."

"One thing has been bothering me," I told her, hoping my delay would give the others time to figure out how to get the moonlight back. "Where did the cream go after it poisoned those people?"

She flipped her fingers dismissively. "It is quite useful to have a hobgoblin of one's own, dear. They can get in and out unseen where others couldn't."

That explained the missing boxes of product Mrs. F and the imposter had told me about. "You're diabolical," I said, no longer able to hide my anger.

Franny stepped closer, her eyes narrowing. "Do not presume to lecture me, child. I've walked this earth and many others since well before you were even a possibility in someone's mind. I can extinguish you like a bug."

"Yes. You probably can. But if I'm going to die today, rest assured I'm going to take your artifact with me."

Power thickened on the air. Clogging, biting

power that chewed on my nerve endings and made it suddenly hard to breathe.

The very atmosphere throbbed against my skin, creating a deep whomp, whomp, whomp of sound that swirled the thickening mist through the clearing but never seemed to blow it away.

It wasn't until Hebe looked up that I realized the throbbing sound was coming from wings beating the air.

Hebe lifted her hands and sent actual lightning through the mist, spearing a Brock-shaped form above her head as he dropped right onto her, his claws clasping her wrists and tugging her off the ground.

She shrieked, but the sound had nothing to do with pain and everything to do with rage. Fresh bolts of lightning speared from her fingertips, hitting Brock in the chest and shoving him backward. His wings pounded hard against the air, holding him in place as smoke rose from his dark clothing. "Hurry!" he yelled.

I shook off my horror and threw a bolt of seeking magic toward Hebe, enveloping her in a cocoon of charcoal gray light that lifted her off the ground and pulled her attention back toward me.

Something drifted upward from the folds of her gown and hung on the air for a moment before bolting toward me. I recognized the ballerina figurine and smiled, my hand outstretched to claim my prize.

Hebe roared in rage and seemed to give Brock a shove, sending him flying off into the charcoal sky, where he disappeared from sight.

I had no time to worry about his fate. Hebe had refocused her considerable energy on taking back the artifact I'd managed to pull from her grasp. She lifted a hand, bright gold light pulsing around the outstretched limb, and the figurine started to slide back her way.

There was movement down at Hebe's feet. In the midst of feeding every bit of keeper magic I had into holding onto the artifact, I allowed myself to glance quickly downward to see what fresh nightmare was heading my way.

It was Hobs! He was running toward the artifact, oversized eyes locked on it and his long fingers stretching toward the sky.

A moment of panic hit me. Was he going to take it back for her? Had his allegiance swung back to the evil goddess?

I had no way of knowing, but my gut told me he wouldn't turn against his new friends, even if she'd threatened him with his life.

I had to trust that instinct.

"Grab it, Hobs!" I screamed. "Bring it to me."

The hobgoblin jumped into the air and wrapped his long fingers around the ballerina, hitting the ground and rolling toward the platform with his tiny body wrapped protectively around the figurine.

Hebe prepared to turn her rage on the little creature. I couldn't let her do it. I jumped off the platform and started running, grabbing him up and screaming to my friends on the platform. "Catch!" I threw the hobgoblin into the air and turned away, praying my friends managed to get hold of him before her magic hit.

Hebe's roar of pure rage blasted upward like an explosion, searing the trees at the edges of the clearing and setting the leaves on fire. Smoke billowed from the flaming branches, mixing with the goddess-created mist to further block the moon.

If we didn't get some moonlight we couldn't use the trap Rustin and Deg had created for Hebe.

But I had no idea how to make that happen.

All I knew was that I had to do something. So I gathered up what little energy I had left, and ran at the goddess, hoping to take her down and hold her until the others could come up with a plan to help.

A creature that was low to the ground and light on its feet shot past me. Then another. And another. And a fourth.

I realized as the last one brushed past me with a yowl that it was Wicked and his littermates.

Panic for their safety surged up and the energy inside me flared, burning through my veins.

I was two long steps away from Hebe when the

night shifted behind her and Deg appeared. He slammed his palms together and an intricate web was illuminated just above her head. The web shimmered, spinning once, and then dropped over her, tightening until her hands were locked at her sides.

I'd seen the magic once before, used against Jacob Quilleran. It had ultimately failed then, and the breakage in the strands as Hebe struggled against it told me it would fail again. But the cats arrayed around the goddess, their tiny chests alight with their individual magical sigils.

Deg began to chant in Latin. Mandy and LA joined him, the three of them standing around Hebe with their eyes closed and their fingers dancing on the air. Two more webs, one silver and one gold, formed in front of their hands and dropped to cover the goddess.

The kittens walked in a circle around their prisoner, their sigils pulsing with the rhythm of their steps and their eyes glowing orange.

The second and third webs snugged down over the first and Hebe appeared to be well and truly caught.

I started to relax.

The ground beneath my feet rumbled. Then rumbled again. And shifted so violently I stumbled sideways.

The two witches and the human familiar stumbled too. When they fell, the webs they'd created started to blink away in whole patches.

The ground next to me ruptured violently. Dirt and rock shot upward like a geyser. All around me, new ruptures made it impossible to stand, let along perform any kind of magic against the goddess.

"The cats!" I screamed to the witches. "Get them out of here!"

Wicked ran to me, but they grabbed the others and ran for the platform.

Hebe's arms flew up into the air and magic pulsed around her, thick and oozing and white against the night. "Give. Me. My. Artifact!" Her voice boomed around us, each word emphasized by a new eruption in the once-smooth grass of the park.

The ground rumbled again. And again.

Hebe stumbled slightly.

That was when I realized the rumbling wasn't coming from her.

The trees around the clearing seemed to sway. The magic-induced flames extinguishing like candles on a birthday cake, and the night above Hebe sparked with the color of the extinguished flames.

Fire blasted downward, the flames reflected in a thousand glossy scales. The dragon's fire enveloped Hebe, forming a column of flame that turned the ground beneath her feet to char, but seemed only to slither around her like a trap made of fire.

Birte shot past the goddess, her massive silver form barely clearing Hebe's fiery prison. A powerful stroke of her wings carried her back into the sky like an arrow shot from a bow. Hebe rounded her lips and filled her cheeks, and a cool breeze, thick with moisture, consumed the imprisoning column of fire.

As Birte came around for another attack, Hebe threw her hands into the air and sent two thick bolts of lightning spearing toward the dragon.

The bolt hit the beautiful creature in the chest and she threw back her head, screeching in agony as she plummeted toward the ground.

"No!" I screamed, taking a step toward the dragon before jolting to a stop.

Birte was heading right for me. If she crashed into me at that speed, and weighing several thousand pounds, she'd ground me into the dirt before I even had time to scream.

I took off running, praying I'd have time to make it to the pavilion before she hit.

The trees behind me crackled as if struck by more lightning, and the top of one sheared off, collapsing in my direction. It hit the earth right behind me, flinging me to the ground as it bounced into the air from impact and struck the grass mere feet from the platform.

I shoved to my feet again, coughing on the dirt and debris the impact had sent into the air, and stumbled toward the structure.

The ground shook under the force of Birte's hit, throwing me the last couple of feet to the pavilion. I hit the wooden platform and skidded across until I smacked into the picnic tables.

A bolt of lightning hit the protective magics encompassing the structure and the energy was immediately repelled, firing back toward Hebe and sending her soaring backward on a scream. The energy flowed over and through her, turning her muscles rigid and creating a bright, silver aura that flared out around her as she fell to the ground. She didn't stay down long, shoving to her feet, she stood there looking dazed for a beat and then lifted her hands again.

I didn't know if Mandy's repelling spell would work a second time, but judging by the worried expression on the witch's face, I assumed it wouldn't.

"The trap!" Deg yelled as Hebe prepared to hit us again.

A new roar filled the park, deeper and more guttural.

Behind me, someone muttered a heartfelt swear. I turned in time to see Sebille buzzing back to the pavilion. "Where's Rustin? We've been waiting for his okay to light it up."

The clearing was alive with tiny, buzzing figures. Their multi-hued lights sparkling like colored stars across the night sky. The Fae came in for multiple attacks and then danced quickly away as Hebe retaliated.

Rustin appeared next to Sebille. "They need to do it now. Before *that* arrives." He nodded toward the sky-scraper-sized form swaying toward us above the trees.

It was Theo Gargantu. In his true Giant form. *Tyrannosaurus Trousers!* "He's giantnormous!"

Sebille snorted out a laugh. "I have to admit, he gave even mother pause when she first saw him. And when that Itch with a large B took out his dragon girlfriend, I thought he was going to level this whole park. I wouldn't want to be in her ugly, sensible shoes when he reaches her."

"Which is why we need to set the trap sooner rather than later. If he gets caught up in it we're dead. It will never hold them both," Rustin said.

Sebille buzzed off to rally the Fae.

I was dying of curiosity about what they were going to do, but Rustin was a ghost-witch with a mission. He'd already stormed across the pavilion.

Wicked rubbed against my ankles and I picked him up, nuzzling him against my face. "You guys did good work out there, little man."

He purred happily. The other cats ran toward the trap and Wicked shoved me away, jumping down to join them.

They scampered over and spread out, each cat finding the sigil that corresponded to the designs in their chests. I smiled. Deg had helped Rustin design a trap that the cats could amplify with their power.

Now, if we could only get some moonlight on the party...

Light flared above the pavilion amid a loud buzzing sound. I looked up as the silvery glow filtered through the patterns in the roof and painted the floor with magic enhancing symbols.

Queen Sindra's people flared brighter and the symbols started to glow, pulsing with latent energy.

A thunderous cacophony of sound announced Theo's arrival at the edge of the forest. Trees crashed to the ground all around him, ripping the grass and tearing into the adjacent trees as he stepped though, his car-sized fists held down at his sides.

His usually gentle expression turned murderous when he saw the unmoving form of Birte, crumpled near the pavilion.

She'd returned to her human form. I didn't know if that was a good sign or a bad one.

My heart tore as I looked at her, bleeding and scored with electrical burns and lying oh so still.

"Sebille!" I screamed.

In her usual fashion, she ignored me.

I turned my attention to the witches and LA, watching as they sliced an athame across their palms, chanting over the bloody hands as they held them over the symbols and dripped blood over each one.

Fat, white candles flickered around the outside of the trap and their chanting had put the cats into a trance, their sigils glowing again as they stood in their places, unmoving and glassy-eyed.

Theo stomped the ground and roared. Hebe sent a bolt of lightning in his direction but he side-stepped it, surprisingly agile for a creature his size.

His big hand wrapped around the goddess and he lifted her off the ground, lifting her to a spot way too close to his face.

I grimaced. "Please tell me he isn't going to bite her head off or something equally gross?" I prayed to myself. "Please no, please no, please no," I chanted.

Theo opened his mouth and roared right into her face.

Hebe's golden hair flew backward and the skin on her face retreated, making her look like she was staring into a wind tunnel.

Then he shook her like she was a pair of dice in a cup and threw her to the ground.

When Theo lifted his foot to stomp the clearly dazed woman, I screamed. "Theo, look out!"

The witches slammed their palms down on a special symbol at three points in the spell and light flared under their hands. It spread inward, encompassing the carefully drawn sigils and surrounding the cats in a golden glow.

The magic shot upward, flared across the pavilion ceiling and then skimmed downward to coat the open sides and send a layer of golden light across the floor.

It tingled the bottoms of my feet for a beat before it retracted back into the spell and hovered there, spinning slowly as the witches finished their chanting with a shouted power word that gathered the energy and sent it shooting toward the goddess.

Seeing it heading his way, Theo threw the woman into the air and the magic found her, twisting around her like a golden rope and completely encompassing her from her toes to the top of her head.

Hebe fell to the ground in a boneless pile, unmoving.

Silence eased through the structure and filled the clearing.

With an unhappy groan, Theo slowly eased back to his normal size.

The fairies gave up lighting the roof and buzzed down to us.

I caught Sebille's eye and pointed toward Birte. "Help her, please?"

She nodded and buzzed off, followed by the rest of the Fae.

Their light quickly flared as they surrounded the fallen dragon shifter.

Theo knelt nearby, tears glimmering in his gaze.

I looked at my friends and found them drooping wearily on the bench of one of the picnic tables.

"Nice work, you guys."

"We couldn't have done it without Rustin," Deg said. "It was his idea to augment it with blood magic."

I nodded. "Where is he, anyway?"

We looked around, finding no sign of the ghost witch. "He must have gone home." But I frowned in worry. It wasn't unusual for him to disappear like that. But in this case, I would have felt better if he'd let me know he was all right first.

Mr. Slimy was also MIA. Wicked and the other kittens were chasing each other around the tables, pouncing on the occasional unsuspecting cricket.

A cheer went up and I glanced over to find Birte sitting up, blinking in confusion.

I caught Theo's eye and gave him a thumb's up.

A tiny hand touched my arm. I turned to find Hobs looking up at me, his expression sad. He held out the figurine. "I promised."

Nodding, I took it from him. "You did promise. And you kept your promise. Thank you, Hobs. I owe you one."

He nodded, sniffling. "You're welcome. You gave me my freedom and a place to stay. I'm grateful." He turned away, his head hanging low.

I realized in that moment that he thought I would send him away because I'd gotten what I wanted from him. What a horrible life he must have had. "Hobs, don't leave."

He turned hopefully, his eyes still swimming with unshed tears. "You need Hobs to do something else?"

I smiled. "I do."

He looked almost disappointed. "Oh. Okay."

I touched his shoulder. "I want you to stay at Croakies and keep Wicked and Slimy out of trouble. Do you think you could do that?"

His oversized eyes closed and he seemed to suck air in a slow, deep breath. A single tear slipped down his cheek before he looked at me again. "I can do that."

I squeezed his tiny arm. "Good. I'm glad."

"Hey, hobgoblin!" Hobs looked up to find Sebille standing next to a teeter-totter in the nearby playground. She jerked her head at the equipment. "I'll bet you three sprinkle-covered donuts I can send you flying ten feet off the end of this thing."

Hobs bounced up and down, clapping gleefully. "Fifteen feet?"

Sebille let her smile widen. "If you can do twenty I've got a brownie with your name on it back at Croakies."

He squealed with delirious happiness and ran in her direction.

Laughing at them, I shook my head.

"You need a ride back home?" LA asked.

"No. But thanks for all your help. I owe you guys big time."

LA gave me a weary hug. "Don't worry about it. I'm sure I'll think of some way for you to repay me."

I watched them leave and then remembered Grym. I quickly dialed Lea. When she answered, I spoke before she could. "Please tell me he's okay."

"He's much better. Madeline made it back and she's checking him over now. It appears we got most of the magic out of his system."

My smile slid away. "*Most* of it? What about the rest? Is it going to cause him any more problems?"

"We're just not sure. Madeline thinks he can stay ahead of it by taking his true form once a week or so. But we'll keep working on it. The artifact you retrieved might clear it right out of his system. We just don't know."

She was right. I'd forgotten about our plan to reverse the spell with the artifact. "Good. I can't thank you enough for your help, girlfriend."

She laughed. "Yes you can. You can take this kitten to your house tomorrow. She's bouncing off the walls. It's like she thinks she's missing out on something. She's been driving me crazy."

I knew exactly why Hex had felt the need to be somewhere else. "I think she's going to feel better shortly." I told her about LA and the witches. "They plan on stopping by."

"Icicles!" Lea exclaimed happily.

I shook my head. "Hey, Rustin didn't show up there, did he?"

"He's working on Grym with Madeline. Did you need to talk to him?"

I felt the last bit of tension leave my body. "No. I just wanted to make sure he's okay. He and Slimy disappeared."

"Mr. Slimy's holding court in the pond with Wally."

Wally was Lea's non-magical bullfrog.

"He keeps trying to get Wally to talk but it's not happening." She laughed.

"Poor Wally," I lamented. "I'll talk to you in the morning?"

"Sure. Unless you want to bring Wicked by for the kitty party?"

"Not tonight. But thanks." All I wanted was to take a long, hot shower and go to bed. I was beyond beat.

There was a loud thump behind me, followed by happy shrieking and a shrill shout that made me smile.

"Again!"

My cell rang. I answered it without looking at the ID, assuming it was Lea again. "What did you forget?"

A brief silence met my question. And then, "Naida Griffith?"

"This is Naida. Who's this?"

"It's Katherine Geras. Would you mind telling

me why you sent me a picture of my guards in pink tutus?"

Oopsies! "Uh, yeah, about that…"

"*Again!*"

The End

READ MORE ENCHANTING INQUIRIES

Did you enjoy Gram Croakies? If so, you might want to check out Book 5 of *Enchanted Inquiries*, **Croakies and Scream.**

Please enjoy Chapter One of **Croakies and Scream** as my gift to you!

Okay, I'll admit it, this is my least favorite time of year. Yeah, I understand the magic of the season...I get that...but most people don't have jobs that involve wrangling magic. During the last three months of the year magical influences run rampant. And that means a lot more work for me.

And this year is the worst of all.

Why, you ask?

Because I'm not only trying to wrangle the out-of-control magic artifacts flying around all over the place. This year, I also have to try to keep a magical cat and a talking frog out of trouble.

Goddess take the wheel.

Things are about to get really ugly.

CROAKIES AND SCREAM

"Watch out!"

I ducked just in time to keep from getting hit by Nurse Ratchet's bedpan. The nasty curve of dented and pocked metal shot past where my head had been and clanged into the wall, clattering down onto my sales counter as Sebille leaped the magical vacuum cleaner currently trying to suck up Mr. Slimy and smacked the bedpan down as it tried to rise again.

I grabbed the frog, giving him a smile that I hoped would help his eyes sink back into his head before they popped out, and hurried over to dump him into his fish tank for protection.

"Incoming!" Rustin's voice shouted and I turned to find Blackbeard's sword skimming through the air, SB the parrot riding its hilt and painting the air around him blue.

I ducked sideways as the sword slashed toward my heart and reached out, clasping the hilt and sending SB into the air on another wave of foul language overlaid by bleeps.

The parrot dropped onto my shoulder among a cloud of feathers, huffing out a breath as I fell backward, my knees finally giving out on me.

"Avast ye, Lass. Tis the bleepin' devil's own stirrin' the bubblin' cauldron this eve. We'll be blessed ta find the bleepin' back end of the moon without losin' our bloody tail feathers to a bleepin' magical trickster."

I sucked air, watching as Rustin wrangled a golden theater mask that kept trying to fix itself onto his ghostly face. I knew I should go help him, but I needed a minute to gather my breath and count all my fingers and toes.

"Time check!" I yelled, praying the response would be the right one. It had been a long eight hours and I didn't know how much energy I still had in me.

The mask thwacked onto Rustin's face, sending him reeling backward to smack against a bookshelf and send several magical volumes tumbling to the floor.

The vacuum locked onto the pile of books and took off in that direction, putting Berbie the Loving Bug to shame with its speed and maneuverability.

With an alarmed squeal, I threw myself onto the

machine just before its sucky parts glommed onto the books and inhaled them whole into its insatiable bag.

I'd already lost two tea cups, one bank deposit bag, thankfully empty of cash, my favorite pair of sneakers, a bagel with cream cheese and strawberry jelly, a hairbrush, and we'd almost lost Sebille's giant bag to the machine. We would have lost it too, if all three of us hadn't jumped in to hold onto the bag and wrestle the rabid vacuum to the ground. Sebille had yanked the frayed plug from the wall at that point and we'd all taken a deep breath in relief. She'd shoved her bag into a cabinet and closed the door on it, just as the vacuum's cable had lifted off the ground and inserted its plug into the wall again.

It had been a downhill battle for sanity ever since.

Rolling violently beneath me, the vacuum shoved itself off the floor, nearly managing to unseat me in the process, and fought my tightly wrapped arms to get to the books.

"Time!" I shrieked, sweat pouring down my temples and my last nerve unraveling before my very eyes.

"Ten, nine, eight..."

I gritted my teeth and held on.

"Seven, six, five..."

Sebille skidded past, a dancing mop in her arms

and her red hair sticking up as if she'd snacked on a lighted bulb for dinner.

"Four, three, two..."

The world dipped and whirled. The magic-drenched engine beneath me roared, and Sebille's head hit the wall with a hearty, whack, whack, whack as the mop gave it everything it had and then some.

"One!" Rustin screamed.

Nothing changed for a moment. I was still being beaten to a pulp by the determined vacuum. Sebille's head was still denting my wall. And Rustin peered through the front window through the eyes of the golden mask, which was clinging to his wispy countenance as if it had been magically glued there by Elmer the glue god himself.

The dividing door slammed open and Wicked shot through on a yowl, Casanova's chair hot on his heels. The chair stopped in the middle of Croakies, turned this way and that, assessing its targets, and then shot right at Sebille, slamming into her just as the sun rose over the horizon and everything went quiet and still.

I dropped to my butt on the carpet, sneezing as the vacuum coughed out its last, dusty breath. Sebille collapsed under the chair's attack on the back of her knees and sighed, momentarily glad for the chance to rest.

It didn't last long. She soon started shrieking and

shot to her feet as the chair no doubt molested her and then took off across the store, dancing from leg to leg in obvious pleasure of its coup.

A final, alarming clang announced the theater mask's landing on the table beneath the window.

I scrubbed the back of my hand over my brow, mopping up sweat, and let the breath heave through my lungs. "I'm just going to come right out and say it. I hate Halloween."

Sebille shoved the mop to the floor and leaned against the wall. "Amen and amen."

I looked at Rustin. Around midnight, when the mystical veil restraining magic had first dropped, he'd had a few minutes to enjoy being almost fully formed. I'd enjoyed seeing the look of wonder on his face as he examined his hands and looked down at his feet, which were actually touching the carpet. Unfortunately, his pleasure had been blasted away ten seconds later by the herd of ghost bison running from two spectral American Indian warriors on painted ponies.

If I squinted, I thought I could still see the hoof-prints compressing his wispy form.

I shoved to my feet with a groan. "I'm going to bed. I'll see you guys in a few hours."

Sebille nodded. "Don't expect to see me before three this afternoon. I'm going to need serious fudge ripple and peanut butter heaven ice cream therapy to get over being made a sex object by that ferking chair again."

I felt my eyes go wide. "You have ice cream?"

She pasted a glare on her pale, freckled face. "Don't even think about trying to beg some. It's going to take every last spoonful of my stash to recover from last night."

I didn't have it in me to fight. I headed toward the dividing door, yawning widely. "Will you check the locks and wards?"

Sebille grunted her agreement and I started up the stairs to my apartment. A moment later, soft footfalls behind me announced Wicked's arrival. He shot past and slipped through the apartment door, which I'd given up on closing since my cat always opened it again anyway.

The sound of wings fluttering above my head reminded me I hadn't returned the artifacts to their assigned spots. With a weary groan, I turned and flung out a hand, sending my seeking energy toward SB. "Take the sword with you," I told him, my jaw cracking under another yawn.

"Fair seas to ya, Lass."

I saluted him.

A beat later, the mop and the vacuum cleaner floated through the door on a wave of green energy. Sebille trudged through after them, heading toward the spots on the shelves from which the magic had pried them loose. It occurred to me that I could follow her and see where she'd moved her stuff.

I hesitated, torn by warring desires to drop into bed versus finally discovering where Sebille was resting her fiery red head these days.

Eventually, weariness won out and I trudged upstairs, praying the following night would be better than the last. A prayer that wouldn't be answered.

The coming midnight would be Halloween eve, and the magic veil would be the thinnest it had been all year.

Nothing good was gonna come from that.

Check out the entire series here: https://samcheever. com/books/#enchanting

ALSO BY SAM CHEEVER

If you enjoyed **Gram Croakies**, you might also enjoy these other fun mystery series by Sam. To find out more, visit the **BOOKS** page at www. samcheever.com:

Reluctant Familiar Paranormal Mysteries
Yesterday's Paranormal Mysteries
Gainfully Employed Mysteries
Silver Hills Cozy Mysteries
Country Cousin Mysteries

ABOUT THE AUTHOR

USA Today and *Wall Street Journal* Bestselling Author Sam Cheever writes mystery and suspense, creating stories that draw you in and keep you eagerly turning pages. Known for writing great characters, snappy dialogue, and unique and exhilarating stories, Sam is the award-winning author of 80+ books.

To learn more about Sam and her work, visit her at one of her online hotspots:

Website | Facebook | Twitter | Goodreads | Blog |
Text Alert Signup